William D Kempton

Star Dust

Satire, humor and pathos, in prose and verse

William D Kempton

Star Dust
Satire, humor and pathos, in prose and verse

ISBN/EAN: 9783337411480

Printed in Europe, USA, Canada, Australia, Japan

Cover: Foto ©Andreas Hilbeck / pixelio.de

More available books at **www.hansebooks.com**

STAR DUST

SATIRE, HUMOR AND PATHOS

IN PROSE
AND VERSE

BY

WILLIAM D. KEMPTON

("Star" of Porkopolis.)

———————

The loud laugh *may* "speak the vacant mind,"
   But freer far are such from guile
Than him of whom it can be said:
   He never yet has cracked a smile.

THIS BOOK ∴ ∴ ∴

Is not like the rain which falls alike on the just and 'the unjust. Oh, no, it is quite different. The unjust shall no longer get all the good things in life, for this book is to be sold only to those having a good moral character.

Price, Bound in Cloth, One Dollar.

If you can not get it of your bookseller, send your dollar to

WILLIAM D. KEMPTON

53 W. Ninth Street,   **CINCINNATI, OHIO.**

Dedication.

-- -- -- -- -- .. -- .. --- ---

The casting about to find some one to act as a sort of Godfather for this work has given the writer more trouble than has the writing of the whole book. His first intention was to select a victim from his many friends, but the difficulty in deciding on which one, and the fear that in so doing he might estrange the affections of all the rest, caused him to change his mind. He next turned to a number of living celebrities of sufficient prominence to deserve the compliment, but was confronted by another difficulty: the one selected might at some future time be guilty of conduct which would cause the writer to regret his selection. He then began to look for some one so thoroughly dead as not to be open to this objection; but here was a new difficulty. Those whom he first hit upon had already had enough honors of that kind conferred on them, but he finally found one to whom the world owes a great deal, but who nevertheless in this respect has been shamefully neglected. This fact, and not the one that he is a distant relation of the writer, has caused him to dedicate this work to our common progenitor, Adam.

PREFACE.

IN old works on domestic medicine may be found prescriptions containing a formidable array of ingredients, on the theory that some one will be sure to hit, which are known as "shotgun prescriptions."

The following collection of sketches is somewhat on that order. In apologizing for them, however, the author does not urge lofty motives as an excuse for calling the attention of the public to them. On the contrary, he wishes it distinctly understood that they are some of the fugitive productions of idle moments, and are intended for amusement only. If, therefore, their perusal should cause anyone for even the brief space of a half hour to forget the cares and annoyances incident to the struggle for existence in which we are all engaged, the author will feel that they have not been written in vain.

WILLIAM D. KEMPTON.

TABLE OF CONTENTS.

AND OTHERS.

Of Interest

to Cyclists.

AN ODE TO YE UBIQUITOUS SPRINKLERS.

A PARODY.

Sprinkle, sprinkle, Water-cart,
When I wander where thou art;
If the roads be nice and dry,
Always let the water fly.

"When the blazing sun is set,
And the grass with dew is wet,"
Then the roads your soul delight,
For they're sloppy all the night.

Then when I am in the dark,
And the mongrels round me bark,
I hardly know "which way to go,"
On the road you've sprinkled so.

Then, the mud which fills the holes
Through which my spattered cycle rolls,
Makes me hope with all my heart
That from this world you'll soon depart.

"AS OTHERS SEE US."

Sitting by the roadside near Springdale, O., were two of the most forlorn-looking dogs Hamilton County had ever seen; one a large, nondescript animal through whose veins coursed the blood of perhaps a thousand different breeds, the other a scrawny, mangey, sore-eyed skye terrier, who, just as the contestants in the road race whirled past, was heard to say to his companion:

"Why is the man wearing that gray cap in such a hurry?"

"Oh, he's afraid he'll be beaten by the fellow with the corduroy pants, the sweat from whose brow is making the road so muddy, and the one with the red face who

forgot his stockings. He needn't be afraid of him with
the lump on his forehead, nor of him with a boil on his
cheek, as neither are in condition. Just look at that
pretty man with the high shoes! The last time he came
through here he turned the heads of all the girls so that
now every single one of them has a wry neck. But the
fellow with the black hair and dark eyes is the best of all,
for his voice is as gentle as the sighing of a zephyr, as soft
as the cooing of a dove, and as sweet as the gurgle of
molasses from a jug, and when he sings the very birds
stop and listen."

" Why doesn't he sing now ?"

" Dunno. Just look at that old man with the whis-
kers! He wouldn't work that hard if he were paid a
hundred dollars a day. Yet he is nearly killing himself
now just to get to wear the club medal for four months;
and still they say dogs haven't any sense! I'm glad I'm
a dog, aren't you?"

" Well, I should —"

The rest of his remarks were lost in the distance.

AN AUTOGRAPH.

When Time has touch'd thy shapely head,
    And whiten'd thy flowing beard ;
When in thy broad and handsome brow
    Deep furrows have appear'd ;
If then, dear Tom, on memory's page
    My name shall still be found,
Recall, I pray, the pleasant hours
    That we've together found ;
The hills that we've together climb'd,
    Together, coasted down ;
The chickens and the milk consum'd
    At dear Miamitown.

THE DECAYING VILLAGE.

When the railroad was in its infancy, and travel was restricted to the canal-boat and stage-coach, there flourished within twenty-five miles of "Porkopolis" a certain village, which, as it now lies remote from the present highways of commerce, is in an advanced state of senile decay. The population, never large, has gradually diminished and, like the rickety fences, seems in need of support. Here is a vacant house, the remnants of whose clapboard roof are covered with moss and lichens; there a small structure with the weather-boards gone in places, revealing the hewn logs that, no doubt, not only sheltered the pioneer from the fury of the elements, but from hungry beasts and bloodthirsty savages as well; across the way a solitary brick house with blinds minus many slats and innocent of paint; just beyond a more pretentious edifice, probably once the abode of the local Crœsus, but now its rotting veranda bears the weather-beaten shingle of that social oracle, the village doctor.

As the wheelman, after passing through this place, dashes down a grade and into another village with very modern buildings so freshly painted, with lawns so smoothly shaven and walks so painfully regular, he can not help comparing it to the successful man who, in his struggle for wealth, has pushed aside his more deserving competitor, and left him to die in obscurity.

A GREETING.

(From Programme of Tenth Annual Meet of Ohio Division, L. A. W.)

To the L. A. W. members
In the grand old State, Ohio,
Where the fierce, untamed *Coshocton
In the Branches of *Muskingum,
Shrieks a loud and bold †Defiance
To the wild-eyed *Tuscarawas ;
Where the gentle *Ashtabula
Crouches low with fear and trembling
As the grim old *Cuyahoga
Shakes the earth in rage and anger ;
Where the turbulent *Scioto
At the feet of †Chillicothe
Pleads in vain the burning passion
That consumes his heaving bosom ;
Where the beautiful *Miamis
Side by side, like happy lovers,
Down the valleys slowly wander,
Building castles light and airy ;
Where the *Maumee sweetly singeth,
As she glides along so gently,
Songs of love so soft and plaintive
That our hearts are touched with sadness ;
Where the rushing, roaring *Hocking
And the dashing young *Sandusky
Laugh and scorn the feeble moaning
Of the melancholy *Auglaize ;
Yea, to each and every member
In the dear old State, Ohio,
Do the Cincinnati wheelmen
Extend a warm and cordial greeting.

---

*Rivers in Ohio.   †Cities in Ohio.

THE ONLY TRUE HISTORY OF CINCINNATI.

(From Programme of Tenth Annual Meet of Ohio Division, L. A. W.)

Cincinnati, the oldest city in the United States, was founded A. D. 1007, by Thor Finn, who, following in the wake of Lief the Fortunate, landed on the coast of New England, and at once started inland on a tour of discovery. After suffering many and untold hardships he and his followers reached the headwaters of the Ohio, down which they floated till they reached the site of our city. Impressed with the fitness of the location and the picturesqueness of the surroundings, Thor Finn immediately founded a city, to which he gave the name of "Porkopolis." It grew and thrived till the year 1494, when Mr. C. Columbus, while hunting in the wilds of Kentucky, learned—very much to his surprise—of its existence, and forthwith pillaged and destroyed the city and put to death its inhabitants. Not satisfied with the perpetration of this diabolical act, he made his followers swear never to mention the circumstance, which may account for the silence of historians on this subject. A little over a century ago the city was rebuilt, and now, though it has neither a Washington Monument, a Statue of Liberty nor an Obelisk, yet there are many objects to attract and interest the visitor. Five magnificent bridges span the Ohio and bind her to her children, Covington and Newport. Scattered about the city are numerous evidences of the sculptor's art, the most striking of which is the Tyler-Davidson Fountain, the finest in the world; Music Hall, the munificent gift of Reuben Springer, seats six thousand and contains an organ with six thousand pipes ; Eden Park, with the Art Academy and the West Art Museum ; Burnet Woods Park, a square mile in extent ; the Zoological Gardens—these and a thousand and one other attractions that the Wheelmen of Cincinnati will only be too glad to point out to you.

THE LAST LAY OF THE MUDHOLE.

As humble, as meek and as low
　As the plant that blooms in the shade,
Here at the foot of this hill
　For many a long month have I laid.

How often by great heavy wheels
　Has my bosom been crush'd and bruis'd,
By the horses' sharp iron shoes
　Been torn and sadly contus'd.

At last I have had my revenge—
　Revenge that was sudden and sweet
As the rain that follows a drouth,
　Or a foe's unexpected defeat.

Up o'er the crest of the hill,
　All dressed in a suit of blue,
Comes a jaunty young bicyclist
　On a wheel that is bright and new.

See, o'er the handles he throws
　Those l—s so shapely and plump,
As he casts an amorous glance
　At the milkmaid working the pump.

Oh, see, in my bosom he lands;
　My bosom all covered with mud:
Then hear how he strikes the ground
　" With a dull and a sickening thud."

Oh, see on his face so marr'd
　That woebegone look portray'd,
As he picks himself up and hears
　The scornful laugh of the maid.

A CHRISTMAS STORY.

One night, just a week before Christmas, as little Gottlieb Blitzenstrahl lay all alone in his bed, wondering what treasures Santa Claus had in store for him, and had thought of everything from a nimble jack which could be bought for a cent, to a pony and cart, without being able to decide what he wanted, or, rather, what he did not want, a window at the foot of his bed was softly raised.

Startled by the sound, soft as it was, Gottlieb quickly drew the bed clothes over his head and lay there for several moments, expecting every instant to be carried bodily away by either a ghost or a burglar.

No such calamity resulting, however, his alarm soon subsided, and, peeping out from under the blankets, he saw at the open window a chubby little fur-clad dwarf pointing toward something in the yard below.

Reassured by the pleasant smile which lit up his rosy face, and being somewhat curious to know just what might be outside, Gottlieb crept out of bed and cautiously approached the window.

No sooner had he caught a glimpse of a sleigh with a team of reindeer than he was whisked out of the window by the dwarf, who, after quickly wrapping him up in a robe of bear skin, and placing him in one corner of the sleigh, climbed in after him, and giving his team a signal, they were off like a flash.

Noiselessly they flew along, now over the housetops, now past a church where the people were gathered in worship, now past houses through the windows of which they could see little children peacefully sleeping, now over the icy bosom of a river, now far up in the air over a great city, whose many lights looked like a handful of diamonds sprinkled over the ground. On, on they flew till a star appeared in the distance, small at first, but gradually growing larger till it was no longer a star, but an immense icy palace, lit up by millions of little wax candles.

As they draw up before this strange building the doors swing open and little Gottlieb and his captor enter.

This must surely be heaven, thought little Gottlieb, as he viewed with astonishment the mountains of ice cream, the pyramids of delicious cake, the apparently unlimited supply of nuts and fruits, and the endless variety of toys.

For a few moments he stood as one bewildered, and then, with eyes so widely opened that it seemed impossible for them ever to be closed again, he began in an ecstacy of glee to run from one object to another, exclaiming, "Oh, don't I wish I had that! Oh, don't I wish I had this! Oh! Oh! isn't that nice! Oh my! wouldn't I like to have that!" as his eyes fell now on a fiddle, now on a drum, a sled, a pair of skates and a thousand other articles so dear to the heart of the small but vigorous boy.

Thus he ran to and fro, till suddenly he came to a stop before a handsomely nickel-plated boy's safety bicycle. Fiddles, drums and skates were immediately forgotten. He had eyes for nothing else. Wasn't it a beauty? Real rubber tires, just like a man's wheel! A real bell that would ring! How springy the saddle! How shiny the handle-bar and spokes! And then the tool-bag! A real wrench and a screwdriver! An oil-can that would *not* leak! Was there ever anything so wonderful? Oh, that was just what he wanted!

No part of the machine escaped his scrutiny. He applied the brake, examined the chain and twirled the pedals; but just as he squeezed the oil-can a jet of its contents struck him in the eyes, and he felt so drowsy that he would have fallen to sleep on the ground had he not been picked up by the dwarf and again placed in the sleigh.

On awaking next morning he was greatly surprised to find himself in bed. He sprang to the floor and ran to the window, but neither track nor hoof-print were to be seen.

Puzzled in the extreme, he donned his clothes and went to breakfast. Much to his mother's alarm he left his food untouched. At school he saw safeties on every page of his books, and even the figures on the blackboard went through the performance of some 'very queer maneuvers.

When Saturday came and he went down town to look at the windows of the toy stores, he saw in one of them the exact counterpart of that safety, and the more he looked at it the more certain he became that he was destined to own that very identical machine; and oh, how impatiently he counted the hours that must elapse between that time and Christmas morning.

Never did a boy look forward more eagerly to that morning, never did time pass so slowly, and never was a boy more certain as to what the day would bring forth.

The night before Christmas at length arrived, and after hanging up his stocking and placing two chairs beneath it to receive the bicycle, little Gottlieb crawled into bed, firmly determined to lie awake till his presents arrived; but like a great many other little boys who have tried the same experiment, he was soon fast asleep.

When he awoke he saw that Santa Claus had come and gone while he slept, for on the chairs, in full view, were a bag of candy, a silk handkerchief, a pocket knife with a pearl handle, some oranges and nuts and a handsomely bound gilt-edged Bible. "Only these and nothing more."

THE CYCLOMETER'S VICTIM.

In a great Western city
Lived a man, tough and gritty,
With a love for cycling intense;
He could climb any grade
That ever was made,
Then boast of feeling immense.

Alas! what a pity
This man, tough and gritty,
At last should be so undone!
A cyclometer prize
Did dazzle his eyes—
He raced like the D—ickens and won.

After each long trial
He'd look at the dial,
And say to his friends, " What fun !"
But still it cried more,
Till he finally swore
He'd start on a century run.

With his cycle beside him
In a heap they did find him,
By the side of the road where he laid ;
Then read his cyclometer,
As did the thermometer,
One hundred and one in the shade.

"TIME WORKS WONDERS."

Once upon a time there sat by the side of the road, on an exposed root of a honey locust tree, a widowed tumble-bug. As she wiped the tears from her eyes with a dainty hemstitched handkerchief, made from the finest spider-web, she was heard to say to a fuzzy red caterpillar close by:

"No, I shall never find another like him. He was always so kind and considerate. He was so afraid I would overdo myself, that when we came to a steep place, as we were rolling the ball along, he always took the lower side and insisted on my taking the upper, and it was then that that wheel, with that dreadful man on it, came along and crushed the life out of him. Oh! Oh! I know I shall never find another like him!"

"I know it is sad," sympathized the caterpillar. "I have often envied you when I noticed how attentive he was, for I have never known what it was to have either father, mother or companion. I have frequently wondered how I should feel to have some one to care for me as he cared for you. I feel so lonesome at times I can hardly eat, and am often in need of sympathy."

"Tut! Tut!" exclaimed a large and vicious-looking gray spider, "worry over a husband? Why, they're the greatest nuisances in the world. But why don't you get revenge for his death?"

"What can I do?" sobbed the young widow.

"Well, you can't do much, that's a fact," said the sarcastic spider, "but I'll do what I can for you. I'll hang from that limb that reaches over the path, and when the next one of those fellows comes along I'll give him a bite that will make him fall to the ground, and—"

27

"Good! Good!" shouted a hornet, as he sharpened his rapier on a pebble, "that's the way to serve 'em! Teach 'em to be a little more careful in dealing out death and destruction as they ride about the country. I'll help you in the good work. I'll get my brethren to assist me. We'll investigate his hosiery; we'll perforate his knicker-bockers; we'll give him the Odd Fellows' grip; we'll raise Indian mounds on his forehead and make him behold the most brilliant pyrotechnical display he ever saw in his life."

The next wheelman who passed that way would no doubt have fared badly, indeed, had not the widow fortunately found another companion, the hornet forgot his appointment and the spider been gobbled up by a Thanksgiving turkey.

*TO OTHERS.

To you who smile when you hear our name
    And think some other better,
Pray read this truthful narrative,
    And its moral carefully ponder :
'Tis said there was once a man who owned
    A mangey, sore-eyed doggy ;
'Twas minus a tail and one front leg,
    And was altogether " groggy."
This canine's life the wanton boys
    With sticks and stones tormented,
Till, finally, the aforesaid man
    Their cruelty resented ;
And so to make them all respect
    This noble mongrel scion,
And strike with fear their coward hearts,
    He called the poodle LION.

*From the Hand-Book of The "Porkopolis" Wheelmen
for 1890.

MIAMITOWN.

What place to wheelmen's hearts so dear,
So well deserves renown
For charming scenes and such good cheer,
As quaint Miamitown?

At a point fifteen miles northwest of Cincinnati, where the Cincinnati and Harrison Turnpike crosses the placid Big Miami River, lies a sleepy little hamlet, which the postoffice authorities call Miami, but which the wheelmen of Cincinnati persist in calling Miamitown.

In 1816, when the Big Miami was still a navigable stream, a dam was built, a mill erected, and the village founded. For a time all went well, the population increased and the citizens began to look on their village as a possible future metropolis.

The gradual shoaling of the river and the building of railroads that did not pass through Miami soon diverted to other channels the trade and commerce that had stimulated her growth, and it was not long till, like the hibernating animal, she sank to sleep.

The population has diminished one-half, and not a few of the houses have decayed and been destroyed. The small windows of the old mill look out over the river no longer. In 1887 it was remodeled and modernized, and now looks as ill at ease as the laborer in his Sunday clothes.

On the bank of the river, within a stone's throw of the mill, is a small, rude structure, whose clapboard roof and walls of rough and illy-fitted boards suggest the abode of poverty and want. The interior, with its backless wooden chair, its decrepit stove, its ancient bureau, its feeble and rickety bedstead, with soiled and tumbled bedding; its uneven floor, littered with fuel, dirt and trash; and the appearance of the solitary occupant, with his low and narrow forehead, surmounted by a mat of grizzled hair, his foxy eyes, his open mouth revealing a few filthy snags, his ragged beard and his patched and seedy clothing, tend but to confirm this impression. From inquiries among his neighbors I learned that his name is Elisha Cleaver, that he was born in Pennsylvania in 1835, and that when quite young he had drifted with his parents to his present location.

As a child, he was said to be odd; as a youth, peculiar; and as a man, queer.

In '61, charmed by the noise of a fife and a drum, he enlisted in Company D, of Fremont's Body Guard, and it is said that during the three years of his soldier-life the whistling of the bullets and the shrieking of the shells were, to his feeble intellect, weird music, inspiring him to deeds of reckless valor.

At the close of the war, his parents being dead, he supported himself by trading in melons, assisting his neighbors, and, in fact, at anything he could get to do.

At present, however, he does very little, as he is laboring under the delusion that, like the Apostle John, he is a "fisher of men."

He makes frequent trips to the city on urgent government business, the nature of which he will impart to no one. It is also said that on dark and stormy nights he may be seen by the lightning's flash standing in the door of his hut, midst the swish of the rain, the howling of the wind, and the crash the thunder, waving aloft an old and rusty sword, as though he were leading the celestial orchestra.

The magnet which attracts such numbers of wheelmen to this place, however, is the bounteous meal served by the genial hostess of the Chambers House. When it is said that the road to Miami is a succession of hills, and that the dinner is one that would tempt the gods, the reader need not be surprised to learn that the wheelmen do such justice to it that their machines are in danger of breaking down under the additional weight.

A bright little five-year-old girl, who had frequently listened to a certain wheelman's account of the delights of a run to Miamitown, was heard to say, "Mamma, when I get big, won't you get me a bicycle so I can go to His-amitown?"

VAULTING AMBITION.

John Durchfall was a dry-goods clerk,
  With manners mild and meek,
Who notions, shirts and collars sold
  At four-and-a-half a week.
Ambition had not stirred his breast ;
  With life he was content,
As to and from his humble task
  He daily came and went.

Alas, this uneventful life
  Was doomed to be disturb'd,
And Johnny Durchfall's *piece* of mind
  To be from hence perturb'd.
He saw, in a window he daily pass'd,
  A sight that fir'd his brain.
He paused to look—went on his way—
  Then came and looked again.

He read on a card, so neatly tied
  To a wheel of antique mold,
How ne'er again so wondrous cheap
  Would such a wheel be sold.
Now, Johnny had the cash saved up,
  But hardly could decide
Whether to buy a suit of clothes
  Or buy the wheel and ride.

At night he scarce could sleep a wink
　　For thinking of the wheel—
By day the need of a suit of clothes
　　He frequently would feel.
The wheel, at length, the victory wins
　　And Johnny quickly flies
To get the cash and then secure
　　That rare and wondrous prize.

The dealer smiled when he made the sale—
　　A very lucky one—
For the wheel ran as hard as any dray,
　　And almost weighed a ton.
But Johnny took no note of this,
　　His heart was filled with pride.
The only thing that worried him
　　Was how to learn to ride.

That night, as he lay on his meagre bed,
　　He dreamed, as ne'er before.
He coasted moonbeams and flew through the air
　　As swift as a meteor.
He rode up the hills and sped o'er the plains
　　For many and many a league.
He rode from morn till late at night
　　Without the least fatigue.

The morning came and Johnny hied
　　To a secluded street,
In order that his first attempts
　　No critic eye should meet.
The handles seized with vise-like grip,
　　His foot upon the step,
He looked to the right and then to the left,
　　And then began to skip.

He hopp'd and skipp'd, and skipp'd and hopp'd,
    And yet no progress made,
He paused to wipe his dripping brow,
    Then sang out : " Who's afraid ?"
At last he gave a sudden spring
    And on the saddle sat,
The wheel stood still, but Johnny lit
    Square on his Sunday hat.

Slowly he picked himself from the street
    And looked at his ruined clothes,
Then tried to staunch the scarlet stream
    Which flowed from his Grecian nose.
He raised the wheel from off the ground
    And painfully limp'd by its side,
As he sorrowfully said to those about :
    " I do not care to ride."

Next day there appear'd on a newspaper page
    A modest little ad,
Which told, in few and simple words,
    Of a bargain to be had
By such as wished to get a wheel,
    Their leisure to beguile,
And how this very desirable wheel
    Had not been ridden a mile.

"WHERE IGNORANCE IS BLISS," ETC.

One warm midsummer day, when the air was full of moisture and the mercury making desperate efforts to reach the top of the thermometer, a solitary wheelman was toiling up a steep, rough and uninviting grade. As dripping with perspiration and gasping for breath he reached its summit, he was met by a team, and as he bounced about over the bumps and ridges in attempting to pass it, the off horse said to the near one: "That does my heart good! Oh, that all mankind might be compelled to toil and sweat over these wretched thoroughfares, that they might realize how our lives are embittered and abbreviated by the parsimony which provides such miserable highways!"

The cyclist was again in the middle of the road, and was with difficulty picking his way over the uneven surface, when he was set upon by a loudly barking cur, and in attempting to divide his attention between the dog and the ruts he suddenly came to grief. "My, what fun!" maliciously exclaimed the dog, as he turned, and seeing the mischief he had wrought, ran through an open gate.

Slowly and painfully the wheelman gathered himself together, climbed into the saddle, and resumed his journey. As he turned off at a cross roads, a dilapidated barnyard fowl, perched on a stump, flapped its wings and cried: "Ha! There goes the voracious glutton who feasts on my offspring! Down with the villain!"

Onward, still onward, our wheelman sped, and as he was coasting a passably fair grade, a bird perched on the topmost bough of a lofty oak, sang to its mate: "See! Here comes one who has fled from the noise and smoke of the crowded city to this secluded vale, that he may breathe pure air and revel in scenes that will make him forget the discomforts of his noisome prison."

Onward, still onward, our wheelman pressed. Alas, all these remarks were lost on him, as he understood the language of neither bird nor beast.

———

ALADDIN'S LAMP.

When I was young and free from guile,
  And believ'd whate'er I heard,
I read the story of Aladdin's Lamp
  And doubted ne'er a word.

And now, when my brow is deeply seam'd
  And people call me old,
I still believe the story true
  No matter what I'm told.

You smile, I see, but then I've heard
  Far stranger tales than that.
I've heard of wheelmen climbing hills
  As steep as Ararat.

Of taking runs so very long,
  In time so very brief,
That Father Time, left far behind,
  Had almost died of grief.

I've heard of feats so marvelous,
  By novices achiev'd,
That I'm convinced, say what you may,
  Aladdin must have liv'd.

A DELIGHTFUL TOUR.

It is now that the cycling tourist, returning from his vacation, delights in recounting to his less favored brethren the many pleasures of his recent trip. We listen, we applaud and congratulate, for many of us are like the galley slave, whose only vacation will be spent in that narrow house built by the sexton. Yet, strange as it may seem, at the conclusion of our daily toil, we often start on extended tours. With sails unfurled and feet on footrests, we are wafted over roads that are smooth and grades that are easy; now beside a stream whose noisy babbling seems to challenge us to a trial of speed; again through a forest where the breath of the flowers, the voices of birds and the umbrageous retreats invite repose; now pausing at an inn, where a banquet more sumptuous than Aladdin ever dreamed of is served by a host who treats us as guests, and will accept no remuneration. Where? Ah, in the Land of Nod.

THE SCORCHER.

Charm'd by the sweet and melodious notes
That pour'd from a score of feather'd throats,
Breathing the hay's delicious scent,
As through the fields my course I bent;
Far down the road I chanced to spy
A man on a wheel which seemed to fly.
As past where I stood, like a rocket he went,
I saw on his face a look so intent;
A look of pain and anxious haste,
That seemed to say, " No time must I waste,"
For blind and deaf to nature's display,
With downcast eyes he sped on his way.
"It must be a case of life and death,"
I said to myself with bated breath;
" At the door of death some dear one is laid,
And he doth haste for medical aid.
Oh fly, thou wheel, with the wings of the wind,
That he that aid may speedily find,
And again to health that lov'd one restore.
Hasten, I pray thee, beg, and implore."

* * * *

Alas, my friends, it was all a mistake,
He was only trying a record to break.
He rode like a fool, and never once stopp'd
Till, his heart giving out, from his wheel he dropp'd
And gave up the ghost on the ground where he lay.
But he beat the record three seconds, they say.

THE ANTIQUITY OF THE BICYCLE.

The origin of the idea embodied in the rear-driving safety is by no means as recent as some would have us believe, for in the writings of Confucius, who was born in the year 551 B. C., is a description of a machine very similar to those now in use, the model of which was destroyed and the inventor imprisoned because the reigning emperor considered it too great an innovation for that conservative age. And again, in the lately discovered tomb of the Pharoah that oppressed the Jews, there is said to be a hieroglyphic representing a safety machine with spade handles. And further, in the recently published translation of Kalevala, an old Finnish poem, occur the following lines :

> " Sailing through the azure vapors,
> Sailing through the dusk of evening,
> Sailing to the fiery sunset,
> Was the ancient Wainamoinen ;
> On a wheel both strong and graceful,
> Made of steel and India rubber,
> Made with balls in every bearing,
> Sailed the ancient Wainamoinen "

THE LEGEND OF THE BICYCLE.

'Twixt the Little and Big Miamis,
Near the mouth of Mak-e-te-wah,*
Sat and smoked a band of Shawnees.
Long they sat in silence smoking,
Till at length a wither'd sachem,
Full of years and ripe with wisdom,
Slowly rose and thus addressed them :
"Hear ye not the distant thunder
Of the storm, that, fast approaching,
Soon will sweep the fated red man
From the place where dwelt his fathers ?
On our shores the hated pale face,
From the land across the water,
Builds his fire and sets his teepee,
And with all his many warriors
Scorns the feather'd bow and arrow ;
For he fights with sticks that speak with
Tongue of fire and voice of thunder.
I am old and weak and feeble,
Soon my sun will set forever,
But there's naught but fire and slaughter
For the children born to-morrow ;
Vain is hope and vain resistance !
Doomed the red man ! I have spoken !"
Scarcely ceased the aged sachem,
When arose their tried physician.
(Squinting eyes and nose distorted,
Crooked limbs and back protruding.)
Known to him were arts mysterious ;
Herbs that cure and herbs that poison,
Charms that heal, and spells that prostrate.

* The Indian name for Mill Creek, a stream which flows through the western part of Cincinnati and empties into the Ohio.

Thus he spoke to those about him:
"Age has made our father timid,
Second childhood is upon him.
Fear no more the hated pale face!
I have wrought a charm so potent
From our shores he soon shall flee."
Turned he then unto his teepee,
Entered it—then reappearing,
Bore a strange, unique contrivance.
Wheels it had of queer construction,
Tires and felloes—fleetest blacksnake
Held by spokes of red deer's sinews.
Frame of grapevine—tough, elastic—
Eagle wings in place of pedals,
Vertebræ of dreaded rattler
Formed the chain conveying power.
While they gazed in simple wonder,
Thus he spoke of his invention:
"O'er the teepee of the pale face
I will hover as he sleepeth,
And shall cast upon his people
Spells to make him wild and frantic,
Make him plunge in deep Atlantic,
Make him leave this land forever."
Seizing then the dogwood handles,
As he breathed an incantation,
Vaulted quickly to the saddle.
Then they gazed and then they wondered,
As he rose above the tree tops,
As he floated off to eastward,
As at length he disappeared.
Then began a patient waiting
For the time of his returning,
For the time that, never coming,
Brought but bitter disappointment.

A REMINISCENCE.

In the dim and distant past, so long ago that I can not now remember the exact date, I became the happy owner of a bicycle, and as soon as I learned how to ride I started off on a tour. I toured and toured and toured, till I reached an uninhabited country where I would have perished with hunger had I not fortunately provided myself with a supply of wiener-wurst.

After wandering through this barren wilderness for several days, I came to Zion's Hill and had just succeeded in surmounting it when my eyes were greeted by the sight of fine roads stretching in every direction, in marked contrast to the rough and hilly roads I had been riding over. Hastening forward, without pausing to catch my breath, I was on the point of entering this elysium by the gateway when I was confronted by an old codger, who sprang from a clump of bushes and exclaimed: "Hi there! You can't come in here without a park badge!"

"You don't say so," says I.

"Yes I do," says he, "and I mean it as sure as my name's Adam!"

"So, you're Adam," says I, "and this is the Garden of Eden?"

"Right you are, sonny," says he, "and you want to move on."

I moved on and kept on moving till I met a solitary wheelman, who, as I dismounted to shake hands with him and inquire the way, asked:

"Are you a member of the League of American Wheelmen?"

"What's that?" says I.

43

"Why," he says, "it's the greatest, grandest, and most glorious organization that ever existed."

"Oh!" says I.

"Yes," says he, "and it will protect and defend you wherever you go."

"Do tell," says I.

"What's more," says he, "the members get reduced rates at all League Hotels."

"Laws sakes," says I.

"Yes," says he, "and we're going to have all the roads made as smooth as a floor."

"Won't that be nice?" says I.

"And you get a paper every week," says he.

"Get out!" says I.

"Yes, sir," says he, "and whenever you come to a town when you are on a tour the people will turn out with a brass band to meet you."

"Well, well!" says I, "and can you get into the Garden of Eden?"

"Of course," says he; "just show your League ticket and old Adam will drop on his knees, knock his forehead against the ground, and say, 'the place is yours, help yourself.'"

"And what does it all cost?" says I.

"Only a dollar," says he, as he drew out some application blanks from his pocket.

"Stop a bit," says I. "A dollar is a sight of money these hard times. I'll think about it a while before I join."

Replacing the blanks in his pocket, we shook hands once more and went our separate ways.

Several years later I attended a meeting of wheelmen in Cincinnati, who were indignating over an attempt on the part of the chief of police to stop bicycle riding on the asphalt streets. Governor Foraker and Mayor Smith were present, and each had something to say, but the one to whom the wheelmen listened with the greatest attention was the solitary wheelman whom I had met years ago.

"Who is he?" says I to my neighbor on the right.

"Why," says he, "that's T. J. Kirkpatrick, Chief Consul of the Ohio Division."

———

A WOULD-BE AERONAUT.

Said a lad who aspired to be a high flyer,
As he saw a wheel with a pneumatic tire,
High o'er the heads of the crowd I could pass,
If the tires were but filled with hydrogen gas.

Straight to the store of the dealer he hies,
And picks out a tire of generous size,
And to further assure the success of his plan,
He adds a monster electrical fan.

When the tires were inflated with hydrogen gas,
The curious public assembled en masse
To see him start on his trip to the skies
And he strained every nerve to make the thing rise—
  but it wouldn't.

THE DRINK QUESTION.

Among the first things acquired on a run by a new rider is a consuming thirst, to quench which he has recourse to different liquids varying in strength from Adam's ale to the juice of the corn.

If he is alone there is nothing to compel him to imbibe more than he wants, but if he has several companions he will almost invariably ask them to drink at his expense, and, as they will insist on reciprocating, he will be compelled to drink more than he wants even if it is no more stimulating than lemonade or ginger ale. When there are but two or three in the party the evil is not so apparent as it is when there are ten or a dozen.

In recognizing this evil and attempting to control it, some bicycle clubs have adopted the plan of collecting a certain sum from each member just before starting on a run, which fund is placed in the hands of the captain who makes all disbursements till the fund is exhausted, when another collection is raised, and so on till the run is completed.

If all of the members of a club were equally inclined to drink, this plan would work to perfection, but they are not and probably never will be. Some drink more than is good for them simply because they are paying for it, and one may drink too much lemonade, seltzer or ginger ale as well as stronger drinks. Again, one who drinks but little may find that he is paying at the rate of a dollar a glass for lemonade, while others are getting their drinks at even less than "League rates."

When the "Porkopolis" Wheelmen organized, over two years ago, the following by-law was adopted: "There shall be no 'treating' between members while on a club run."

While each member by this rule pays for what he consumes he is not prohibited from drinking as much or as often as he wishes, neither is there any inducement for him to drink more than he desires. At the same time it effectually prevents "sponging."

Outsiders who did not understand its import greeted this rule with ridicule and much adverse criticism, but now after a trial of two years it is doubtful if a motion to repeal it would receive one vote.

One noticeable result has been the small amount of drinking; in fact some members have declared that since they have united with the club they have saved more than their monthly dues in drinks alone.

A BICYCLE CLUB

Is somewhat of an anomaly, as it is neither an athletic nor a social organization pure and simple, but is a combination of both, and therein lies its weakness. Without social features there is nothing at the end of the riding season to hold the club together, whilst if this feature predominates the cycles are apt to grow rusty from disuse. In this very feature, however, there is a lurking evil, for unfortunately there are some individuals who can not conceive of a social gathering in which "John Barleycorn" does not participate. There are some such who have contracted, or rather expanded, the habit of drinking till their capacity has become unlimited. There are others who take in such quantities of "fire water" that their wheels become unmanagable, and to whom it might not

be safe to suggest the taking of such loads on the install-
ment plan. The presence of such an element in a bicycle
club may be all right to those who take pride in styling
themselves " men of the world," and who sneeringly
allude to those who think differently as " narrow-minded,"
but it is certainly not calculated to elevate or advance
cycling to any great extent, for the interest of such persons in cycling is generally in an inverse ratio to their
capacity for stimulants.

"WHY DO PERSONS GIVE UP CYCLING

If it is so enjoyable and beneficial?" is not infrequently
asked of the cycling enthusiast, and he is forced to admit
that strange as it may seem that some do actually abandon
the wheel.

Among those who grow weary of the sport is the
would-be scorcher, who seems to be laboring under the
delusion that he will be thought a novice unless he rides
very far or very fast, and who in his anxiety to achieve
notoriety in that direction tears along the road with his
head down, and consequently sees as little of the scenery
as though he were riding through a tunnel. He soon,
however, reaches the limit beyond which he can not go,
and then his enthusiasm subsides as rapidly as a spent
rocket.

Another is he who has worshiped at the shrine of
Bacchus till his face has become as luminous as the Aurora
Borealis. On his dull ears the music of the rippling
stream, the song of the brown thrush and the cheerful
notes of the robin fall unheeded. To his eyes, clouded
by the mists of frequent potations, and to his intellect

blunted by tippling, the beauties of nature possess no attraction. He measures the miles by the number of saloons, and sees no pleasure in a club run unless it is in the nature of a "spree." He soon finds that in the city resorts he can get better liquor with less exertion, and it is not at all strange that his wheel should become covered with dust and festooned with cobwebs.

TO RIDE AT THE TOP OF ONE'S SPEED

And only make stops for the purpose of swallowing stimulants is not the way to get either the greatest pleasure or the greatest benefit from the use of the wheel. The only time when their use is at all justifiable is when it is a case of get there at all hazards. The belief that they add strength to the rider is all a mistake, for he who resorts to them is simply making drafts on his store of vital energy which must be honored the following day. Cycling is a sport that requires a temperate life for its fullest enjoyment. It is utterly incompatible with dissipation of any kind whatsoever, and he who is leading the life that ends in an early grave soon finds that he must either reform or give up the wheel, while to him whose blood is free from alcohol and the virus of disease its proper use is not only a source of pleasure, but enables him to go about his business with a clear brain, invigorated muscles and every organ performing its functions in a healthy manner.

IN HEAVEN.

"What kind of streets does heaven have?"
Said Johnny to his mother;
"Say, are they hilly, rough, or smooth,
And one just like another?"

"They're paved with purest gold, my son,
And level as a table;
They're smooth as polished glass, you'll find,
If you'll but read the Bible."

"Then if I'm good as I can be,
And die and go to heaven,
Say, can I ride a golden wheel
Upon those streets so even?"

"Oh, no, my son, the people there
Will spend their time in singing,
And forevermore that blest abode
With anthems will be ringing."

"Well, if I go there when I die,
And riding is forbidden,
I'll ask the man who keeps the gate
To let me out of heaven."

MEPHITIS.

In 1889, when the president of the L. A. W. proposed to introduce simultaneously into the legislatures of eight different States, bills reforming the methods of making and keeping our highways, his plans were opposed by the writer on the ground that as the rural public were not sufficiently educated to appreciate the necessity of such measures, they would only result disastrously. In taking this stand he was severely criticised by several recent additions to the L. A. W., who were captivated by the brilliancy of the scheme, but the fulfillment of his predictions justified the stand taken and provoked the following:

In reading the inaugural address of Governor Campbell, and failing to discover one word in regard to making and repairing our highways, I am reminded of the following old fable, which I have often, when a child, heard my mother relate: " Once upon a time the skunks assembled in the shadow of a great *Hill. One of their number, who was sleeker, plumper and more glossy than the rest, addressed them as follows: ' Fellow skunks, we have met here to devise means of diminishing the difficulties of obtaining a livelihood. We must unite. We must let the other animals know that we have a very *strong* organization, and if they do not do as we desire we can make it very disagreeable for them. We must compel them to remove the briers that tear our fur, and to beat down for us paths to every rabbit burrow in the country.' The young skunks were loud in their applause of these wise remarks, and when one measly old fellow suggested that the other animals might not be so easily intimidated he was pounced upon and narrowly escaped with his life. The upshot of the whole matter was the appointing of a committee to wait on the †Camel, and tell him what the

51

‡Beaver had done, and insist on him doing likewise. When the committee arrived they found the †Camel surrounded by a band of hungry and clamorous wolves, and were unable either to get themselves noticed or to make themselves heard." The rest of this fable I have unfortunately forgotten.

*Governor Hill, of New York.
†Governor Campbell, of Ohio.
‡Governor Beaver, of Pennsylvania.

A MODERN KNIGHT.

In books which are yellow and musty with age,
　We read of knights who were fearless and brave ;
Who wore iron clothes and rode fiery steeds,
　And cut short the life of many a knave.

This knight of ours was not one of those.
　His steed had four legs, yet 'twas fashioned from wood.
He bestrode it at morn, dismounted at eve,
　Yet it never once stirr'd from the spot where it stood.

His lance was a pen well poisoned with ink,
　Which he skillfully used with such fatal effect
That his fame spread abroad, and wherever he went
　He was sure to be met with the greatest respect.

Alas, for our knight ! His triumph was brief,
　For a legion of imps his weapon defied,
Though he fought them with powders and queer little pills
　And every concoction he heard of was tried.

He fought them in vain and began to despair,
　When some one suggested he try a new steed.
He took the advice and purchased a wheel,
　And no longer's a prey to the pharmacist's greed.

AUTUMN.

When autumn, with her shortening days,
  Proclaims the waning of the year,
'Tis then the wheelman finds delight
  And vigor in the bracing air.

To the wheelman whose muscles are in good condition, and who is willing to rise early and ride slowly, long rides at this season of the year have many attractions. It may, it is true, require the exercise of considerable will power to enable him to leave the embrace of the drowsy god, but the pleasures in store for him more than compensate this act of self-denial. The dim light, the cool, bracing air, the silence that is soon broken by a choral from a thousand feathered throats, all tend to make him forget the drudgery of the past week. And then as it grows lighter the very trees seem to nod a welcome, the rosy-cheeked apples that peep through the foliage to wish him good morning, and every object along the route to bid him good speed.

THE STRIKE OF THE "BIKE."

Though science may teach, and experiment prove
  That pain is unknown to iron and steel,
Yet a tale which I heard and will shortly relate
  Constrains me to think that at least they can feel.

It concerns the fate of a weak-minded lad,
  Whose consuming desire was a record " to beat,"
Who liv'd on his wheel, and though urged by his friends
  'Twas seldom he'd leave it to sleep or to eat.

He rode till even the wheels were tir'd,
  The down-trodden pedals complain'd of their lot,
The many-link'd chain rebell'd at the strain
  And the bearings had grown exceedingly hot.

When forbearance and patience had come to an end,
  They sought out some means to vent their dislike,
And after discussing this plan and that
  They firmly resolved to go on a strike.

He kept on his way and was nearing the goal.
  He flew like the wind and was bent o'er his work,
For he had but a very few seconds to spare,
  When lo : his wheel was stopped with a jerk.

He slid o'er the handles and lit on his head,
  His friends gather'd round to look at the wreck.
The wrongs of the "bike" at last were avenged,
  For instead of the record he'd broken his neck.

THE PUMPERNICKEL BICYCLE CLUB.

You never heard of the Pumpernickel Bicycle Club? Why, that's very strange.

Well, it all came about in this manner. You see there had been a great deal of asphalt pavement laid in different parts of the city, and all the old wheels, no matter how rusty and forlorn looking, were dragged from the obscurity of dusty attics, and after being cleaned and polished till they glistened anew, were given an airing before the admiring gaze of the multitude that crowded the sidewalks.

Not content, however, with simply riding up and down the street and exciting the admiration of the fair sex, some of the riders began to attempt startling feats of daring.

Moses Smashheimer electrified the populace by riding at full speed with Leonardi Sphagetti standing on the step and clinging to the tail of his coat. Patsy Flannigan roused their latent enthusiasm by riding with one foot on the step and the other on the pedal. But when the portly Augustus Limburger actually let go of the handles and folded his arms across his capacious bosom, the spectators could contain themselves no longer. Hats were thrown in the air, handkerchiefs were waved and the air was rent with shouts and cheers.

It was just at this time that the gigantic intellect of Diedrich Rausmitem conceived the brilliant idea of forming a club, and as he was never known to let grass grow under his feet, he lost no time in imparting to his fellow wheelmen the nature of his scheme and the many advantages thereof.

55

As a result of his glowing accounts, a dozen wheelmen congregated about the base of the fountain that very evening and organized the Pumpernickel Bicycle Club. The monthly dues were put at five cents, partly because they did not wish to put on too much style at first, but principally because very few of them earned more than three dollars a week.

The following evening they held an election of officers and chose the dignified Limburger for President, with Rausmitem for Captain, Sphagetti for Secretary, Grabheimer for Treasurer, and Smashheimer for Bugler, and then to prevent any dissatisfaction they made Lieutenants of all the rest.

The club had been in existence for fully three weeks when they came to the unanimous conclusion that in order to be distinguished from the vulgar herd they must have a suitable uniform, and so after a heated discussion, during which the Secretary and Bugler almost came to blows, they adopted a coat and knee breeches of bottle green velveteen, with cap and stockings to match.

The very first Sunday after receiving the new uniforms they sallied forth to be greeted with admiring glances from the fair ones and to be complimented on the very appropriate color of their suits by those wheelmen who were not members of the club. Sunday after Sunday they rode up and down the street displaying their handsome uniforms and shapely limbs to a never-decreasing throng of spectators. Tiring at length of the monotony of this parade they began to look about for new worlds to conquer. It was then that Rausmitem conceived another brilliant idea. He had read in a cycling paper that a certain club had taken a run and that it was the Captain's duty to call the run.

With him, to think was to act, and he forthwith announced to the club that on the next Sunday they would assemble at the fountain at 7 a. m. and take a run to H——. The idea of taking a run met with universal favor, but the destination did not suit them, and so they overruled the Captain and decided to go to B——, which was in the opposite direction and forty miles away. It was their first run, and being very enthusiastic they would be satisfied with nothing less than eighty miles.

They assembled at the appointed time and place. Smashheimer had borrowed a bugle for the occasion, and by its aid produced some of the most unearthly noises to which human ear had ever listened, and when the club started, with the Captain in the lead, he continued his diabolical performance, to the great annoyance of the late sleepers along the route.

All went well till they reached the point where the asphalt pavement ended and the cobblestones began. Before they had gone the distance of a block over the rough surface, Smashheimer's wheel swerved, threw him against the Captain and both came down with a crash, quickly followed by a half dozen others. All was confusion and commotion. Those who had not fallen dismounted at once and stood by their wheels while they called to the others to help extricate the unfortunate ones from the tangle. When the latter finally succeeded in separating themselves it was found that Smashheimer's handlebar was broken off close to the head and that Rausmitem's clothing was plentifully besmeared with mud and filth.

Seeing their captain's sorry plight they began with one accord to poke fun at him, and as he was in no very good humor at being overruled on the destination, it may be imagined that he did not take their raillery in very good part. In fact, he began to talk back, which only increased their merriment and in turn added to his ill humor. Retort followed rejoinder and Rausmitem was on the point of demonstrating his boasted ability to wipe up the earth with a half dozen of them when the President interfered and succeeded in restoring peace. Changing coats with Smashheimer, who was obliged to return on account of his broken wheel, Rausmitem again took the lead.

The pace was necessarily slow and falls not infrequent, but when they reached a comparatively smooth turnpike on the outskirts of the city they unconsciously began riding faster and faster till the run degenerated into a road race. The hot pace soon began to tell, and several of them who had never ridden on anything but asphalt gradually dropped to the rear, and when the first hill was reached they were fully a mile behind the leader. They had become so scattered by this time that it was now every one for himself and the devil take the hindmost. Rausmitem, who would let no one pass him, maintained the lead and reached B—— at 1 o'clock in the afternoon. When Patsy Flannigan came in sight a half hour later it was to be greeted by bantering remarks by the Captain, to which he might have taken umbrage had he not been so thoroughly exhausted that he had to be assisted in alighting from his wheel. Three others succeeded in straggling in before 3 o'clock, hardly able to propel their wheels. As for the rest, some had fallen by the wayside before half the distance had been covered, whilst others had lost their way and floundered along over sandy roads till their muscles, unaccustomed to the unusual strain, positively refused to contract and they were compelled to stop. The five who had succeeded in reaching B—— concluded, after eating their dinner and finding how tired they were, to return by rail. The rest got back the best way they could, some by dint of alternate walking and riding, others by the opportune aid of market wagons on their way to the city.

The initial run having been so disastrous and having made such inroads on their slender purses, it was all of a month before they could muster up sufficient courage to make a second attempt. This time, profiting by experience, they selected a point only fifteen miles distant.

They took an early start and made the usual gallant display as they rode through the city, but when they reached the outskirts they began to scatter as before. Rausmitem, who was first to reach the destination, took a fiendish delight in unmercifully twitting the others as they arrived, one at a time, all of which was well calculated to cultivate a feeling of harmony in the club.

Although they were nearly "tuckered out" from the long ride and stiff pace, they still had strength enough, on hearing the dinner bell, to rush for the dining.room like a pack of famished wolves. The very fierceness of their onset, however, prevented any of them gaining an entrance, for those in advance became wedged in the doorway and could not get out on account of the pressure of those in the rear. They surged and pushed, crowded and squeezed, vociferated and trod on each other's toes all to no avail, and had not the stalwart landlord interfered and dragged them out one at a time they might still be struggling and fighting at that dining-room door.

When they finally did get into the room the fierce onslaught they made on the table appalled even those who were accustomed to cater to the robust appetites of farm hands. Within less than three minutes they had transferred every edible on the table to their plates, for it was not often that they had paid as much as twenty-five cents for a single meal and they proposed to get the worth of their money. They devoured everything in sight, and ever since that day the landlord charges wheelmen fifty cents a head.

The season was now growing late, and their meeting place, the base of the fountain, was not only damp and conducive to colds, but was altogether too well ventilated for comfort. This casued considerable murmuring, and the club was on the point of disruption, when some one suggested that they hire a room where they could have a fire to keep them warm. This proposition met with favor from some, but was strenuously opposed by others, who objected to paying any more dues than they were paying just to provide a loafing place for a few others.

The opposition daily gained strength and the club-room scheme seemed doomed, when it was reported that some envious wheelmen not members of the club had dubbed them the Curbstone Club. That settled the whole matter. They would not rest under such a stigma a moment. They at once raised the monthly dues to twenty-five cents and started the President and the Captain out to hunt for a suitable room.

They finally secured one in the rear of a butcher shop for a monthly rental of three dollars, payable in advance. After they had cleaned up the room each member brought a chair, the butcher loaned them a table and the treasury was drawn upon to pay for a coal bucket and a fire shovel. They then agreed to take turns in acting as janitor, and in that way dispense with the service and save the salary of that autocratic menial.

Their first meeting in their clubroom was celebrated

by a lunch. They had wiener-wurst, pumpernickel and sauer-kraut galore, and it was the first really harmonious meeting they had held since their organization.

A new difficulty now confronted them. The revenue from dues was barely sufficient to pay their rent, and as increasing the monthly dues was out of the question their only way out of the difficulty was to secure new members.

From that time on every wheelman in town was besought to join the club. They were indefatigable in their efforts to secure recruits and gave their victims no peace till they secured their applications. The character of the recruits made no difference, so long as they were able to ride a wheel and pay the club dues. One could not take a ride of a half hour's duration without being repeatedly and persistently urged to join the club. As a result of this ceaseless effort they doubled their membership in a very short time. Their very prosperity, however, added to their troubles, for the increased membership brought a demand for better accommodations and increased expense.

After much wrangling, and frequent and bitter discussion, they raised their monthly dues to fifty cents, and secured an additional room from the butcher. In spite of the increased membership, however, they were not happy. The club was torn by dissensions. Several of those who were compelled to forbear smoking cigarettes, on account of the increase in dues, were loud in their criticism of the action of the club officials, and bitterly denounced the extravagant manner in which the affairs of the club were conducted. The bad feeling between the members continued to increase, and matters were rapidly going from bad to worse, when the gifted Rausmitem again came to their rescue with a brilliant idea.

It was nothing else than holding a race meet, under the auspices of the club. In broaching the scheme, Rausmitem painted it in glowing colors, and showed them that, if properly managed, it would not only add to their glory, and make the name of the Pumpernickel Bicycle Club pre-eminent, but it would also be a money-making scheme. This latter feature turned the balance, and they unanimously resolved to give a race meet.

All was harmony now with a large H. They went to work with a will; they constituted themselves a monster begging committee. They begged medals and prizes of all sorts. They got up an elaborate program, and made the lives of the merchants that they called on miserable till they agreed to take an advertisement.

Everything, even to the music and the grounds, was donated. Then the tickets—each member took a stipulated number, which he agreed to sell or dispose of, and the way they pestered their friends was a caution.

The appointed day came, and, fortunately, the weather left nothing to be desired. The racers came from all directions, for race-meets in those days were none too common. The handsome Limburger officiated as referee, while Rausmitem fired the pistol at the beginning of each race. All the rest of the club were there in some capacity or other, each resplendent in a clean shirt and a gorgeous badge.

The fair sex, who filled the grand stand, were generous in their applause, and when Patsy Flannigan handed out the medals and prizes at the end of each race he was cheered to the echo. The affair was a great success, and the name of the Pumpernickel Bicycle Club was, indeed, famous. What was of more importance, however, was the fact that, after all bills were paid, there remained in the hands of the finance committee just three hundred and sixty-one dollars.

Three hundred and sixty-one dollars! Just think of it! Why that was more than many of them could earn if they worked steadily for two whole years. It was a fabulous sum to some of them. What were they to do with it? Some were in favor of abolishing the club dues and drawing on the treasury for the expenses of the club till the money was exhausted. Others proposed to rent a large house and furnish it elegantly, contending that if they did so they would get thousands of new members, who would rather come to the club and play billiards for nothing, than go to a saloon, where they would have to pay for each game. Others even suggested that the money be used as a nucleus of a fund for the building of a club-house, etc.

Some of the more level-headed members called attention to the fact that their money would not even buy carpets for such a place as they wanted, and asked where they expected to get the money to buy billiard tables and to pay the rent. They were howled down, however. They were old fogies. They had no ambition or enterprise. They did not know enough to come in out of the rain.

With such a large sum in the treasury, and each member advocating a different method of disposing of it, it may be naturally concluded that they were unable to settle on any one plan. Not only this, but they began to call each other names and cast reflections on their honesty. Each one seemed to think the others opposed his scheme because they wanted to get some of the money for their own use. After wrangling and fighting for several weeks over the disposition of the spoils, they finally decided to spend the whole sum on a large supper.

They arranged with a caterer to set out a supper worthy of so prominent a club, and the caterer did his best. He gave them all the delicacies of the season, including twenty-five-cent cigars, ice cream, and drinks of all kinds and strengths. For a short time after they sat down to the tables they were harmonious, but when some of the strong drinks began to have an effect, they began to apply choice epithets and to pelt each other with pieces of bread, meat, and so forth, and, finally, they even threw dishes.

The caterer at this point, fearing that his costly mirrors and handsome furniture might be either injured or destroyed, quietly summoned a couple of patrol wagons, which swooped down on the belligerents and carried them to the stationhouse, where they were permitted to sleep off the effects of their debauch on the hard benches in the cells.

The money having been exhausted and any amount of hard feeling having been engendered, the club was disbanded at the next meeting, and this was the sad end of the once promising Pumpernickel Bicycle Club.

"GOOD LORD, DELIVER US."

From those who carry no oil for their wheels,
    Yet always bother us
And drain our cans of the very last drop—
    " Good Lord, deliver us !"

From those who ask to try our wheels,
    And then will anger us
By riding full tilt over ruts and stones—
    " Good Lord, deliver us !"

From those who ride the "only" wheel,
    And are wont to pester us
By singing its praises for hours and hours—
    " Good Lord, deliver us !"

From the potmetal wheel, though warranted steel,
    Is sure to break under us
Just when we are miles and miles from home—
    " Good Lord, deliver us !"

From these and a thousand kindred ills
    Which still hang over us
And threaten to make us crabbed and cross—
    " Good Lord, deliver us !"

THE ENVIOUS SPIDER.

If I'd tell where I've been,
And the strange sights I've seen,
You would open your eyes
With the greatest surprise—

Sang a gaunt grasshopper, as he swayed to and fro on the top of an iron weed.

"Humph!" snapped a rusty-looking spider from beneath a plantain leaf, "I doubt it."

"You do, eh?" retorted the grasshopper. "Perhaps you have seen a man flying along on two wheels?"

"No, nor has anybody else," sneered the spider.

"Well, I have," simpered a gaudy butterfly from the top of a thistle, "and it gave me such a turn, for as he was admiring my wings the front wheel struck a stone, and, oh my, I thought I should die—"

"It's a pity you didn't, you silly thing," said the spider. "It would take stronger evidence than yours to make me believe it."

"Well, old vinegar face," buzzed a big blue-bottle fly, "you needn't be so spiteful about it."

"What!" screamed the spider, making a spring at the fly. "I'll teach—" but before she could either finish the sentence or get out of the way her life was crushed out by the wheels of one of the very machines whose existence she had doubted.

THE GIFT OF THE GODS.

The Gods and Goddesses all one day,
   From Jupiter down to Pan,
Concluded 'twas time for them to make
   An appropriate gift to man.

But when they came to decide on the gift
   They were all quite badly at sea,
For one wanted this and another that,
   And on none could they all agree.

It began to look like unfortunate man
   The gift most surely would lose,
For the more they argued, disputed and plead,
   The less they were able to choose.

But Jove at length grew tired of the din
   And spoke to Vulcan, his son,
Whom he told to fashion for man a wheel
   That needed no power to run.

Now, Vulcan was bilious and mean to boot,
   And completely soured on man,
So he vow'd, when he started to make the machine,
   He would frustrate his father's plan.

Then he wrought a machine with graceful lines,
   Which the looker-on misled,
But he filled it with friction and bath'd it in sweat,
   And made it as heavy as lead.

And now, when a rider strains every nerve
   To propel his machine up a grade,
This vicious old fellow goes wild with delight
   O'er the trouble for man he has made.

THE SPINNING-WHEEL.

The spinning-wheel our mothers plied
  And fed with wool and flax,
No more will gentler sex enslave
  Or patient fingers tax;
For since it's been "transmogrified"
  It hastes, at her behest,
To carry her through rural scenes
  And add to life a zest.

OUT OF WIND.

When I learn'd to ride a wheel
  I often was chagrin'd
To find, before I'd ridden far,
  That I was out of wind.

I therefore bought a brand new wheel,
  With tires that you inflate,
And hoped this trouble to avoid—
  But such was not my fate.

A piece of wire ran in that tire
  On which my faith I'd pinn'd,
And again I found I could not ride
  Because I was out of wind.

THE RECKLESS COASTER.

With faith in his luck, without bound,
  No coast too steep could be found;
  But he struck a cart end
  As he swept 'round a bend,
And his spirit leap'd out through the wound.

"THERE'S MANY A SLIP," ETC.

At "head work" he was quite an adept;
   He knew all the tricks of the track,
From ankle motion to final spurt,
   Did this wonderful racing crack.

They could not pocket him, he said,
   For he always rode very wide;
But the man who won, like the Levite of old,
   Passed by on the other side.

A SPRING POEM.

Spring, spring, of well temper'd steel,
Absorbing the jolts that we'd painfully feel,
Of chanting thy praises we never shall tire,
Thou gentle hand-maid of the pneumatic tire.

A source of pleasure for age and for youth,
A boon for man and woman, forsooth.
Our mem'ry shall cling as long as we live
To the freedom from jar that thy advent didst give.

AN EPITAPH.

When Death puts forth his clammy hand
   And claims me for his own,
Pray dig my grave in a quiet spot
   And o'er it place a stone.
Engrave thereon a winged wheel,
   And then, beneath, inscribe:
"He loved the wheel, and never tir'd
   It's pleasures to describe."

69

And Others.

THAT CHESTNUT STORY.

A TALE OF WOE IN SIX CANTOS, WITH A MORAL.

CANTO I.

A dark-eyed maiden, so blithe and gay,
Receiv'd, on the morn of her last birthday,
A pasteboard box that was long and slim.
On seeing its shape, she said with a vim,
While her deft little fingers the knots undid
In her eager haste to open the lid,
" Haven't I told them, time and again,
That I didn't want an old gold pen !"
Under that lid—jerked off in a trice—
Cover'd with cotton, so soft and nice,
Nestling together as close and snug
As certain fam'd bugs that were found in a rug,
Were—nothing alive, I'd have you know—
But chestnuts five, all rang'd in a row.
Quickly she spoke: "Who can it be
But that mean old thing, G. W. P.!!!
I'll give him a beating he'll never forget;
I'll do it, too, without a regret;
And feeling the weight of my little fist,
He will think he has rous'd up an anarchist."

CANTO II.

Now, G. W. P., with wide open eyes,
Looked up from the floor, in the greatest surprise,
And begg'd that she would her conduct explain,
And from further punishment quickly refrain.
She impatiently spoke of the chestnuts five ;
But he protested—more dead than alive—
She was laboring under a serious mistake,
And on some one else her vengeance must take.
'' Your cousin, John, I believe is the one,
For he is ever so ready for fun.
And I will aid you to scour this town,
And—when he is found—to do him up brown."

CANTO III.

In a corner stands Johnny, in sore dismay,
So fill'd with surprise scarce a word he can say ;
Aw'd by the flash of her brilliant dark eyes,
To find his lost voice he painfully tries ;
But when he does speak, 'tis to strongly deny
That such a mean trick he ever would try,
And said that he felt in all of his bones
It could be no other than Christopher Jones.

CANTO IV.

With Jack on his feet, and George on his head,
She made poor Christopher wish he was dead,
For while they held him full length on the floor
She pounded him till she could pound him no more ;
And when at length, from exhaustion, she ceas'd,
And Jack and George his person releas'd,

Poor Christy, with clothing all crumpled and rent,
Meekly inquired what all this meant.
Then, with bright, flashing eyes and a rosy face,
She told him right there, before his face,
Of the chestnuts five, which he had sent,
But he stoutly declared he was innocent.

CANTO V.

At this the maiden, sore perplex'd,
And, perhaps, I might say, the least bit vex'd,
Sought out the box with earnestness,
And, patiently studying its address,
Exclaimed aloud : " I do declare,
It's from the girl with the bobtail hair !"

CANTO VI.

She lately had cut from a newspaper page
A peculiar rhyme, in a style now the rage,
That, by means of comparisons very unfair,
Made sport of the girl with the bobtail hair.
This she sent to a friend, who look'd so forlorn,
Because her rich tresses had lately been shorn.
'Twas the fifth she'd received in regard to her locks,
So the chestnuts five she put in a box,
And sent them by mail, without, by the way,
Ever once dreaming that 'twas her birthday.

MORAL.

There is none.

DUDELSACK VS. DOOLITTLE.

On a dirt road that leads off from one of the turn-p'kes radiating from the city of Cincinnati is the Dudelsack homestead.

The house, whose front is guarded by a gigantic old pear tree that spreads out its branches as if to ward off the fierce northern storms, is a large, oddly-shaped building whose windows. no two of a size, and doors of different heights, remind one of nothing so much as of a man dressed in ready-made clothing. no two pieces of which have been bought at the same time or place.

Farther along the road, in a house neither so large nor so odd looking, is the home of Abner Doolittle.

In this out-of-the-way neighborhood there existed one of those organizations, indigenous to small villages, called a literary society. The exact date of its founding no one seemed to know, but all agreed that it was at some very remote period, and that after flourishing for a time it had sickened and apparently died. but had revived on the coming of a more propitious season, and gave promise of a more vigorous growth, only to disappoint the hopes of its friends and again become torpid. Fluctuating thus between the two extremes, it had maintained a precarious existence till the previous autumn, when it had been resuscitated, rechristened, and provided with a new constitution strong enough for a country of even greater size than the United States.

Each of its eleven members was peculiarly fortunate, for in holding one or more of its fifteen offices they were enjoying to the fullest extent the greatest prerogative of an American citizen.

The society had flourished for four whole months, and now, on this first Thursday of the new year, it had met at the home of the Dudelsacks.

Its president had recited "Horatius at the Bridge" with telling effect. Susan Dudelsack had performed the "Blue Danube" on the piano, with impromptu variations. Gottlieb Greenschnable had sung a comic song to an accompaniment played by Arabella Stites. Philip Henry Dudelsack and Ebenezer Doolittle had rendered the scene between Brutus and Cassius with a fervor never before equaled by even the most celebrated actors. Miss Tillie Gump had read an elaborate essay on the duties of woman, and each of the others had creditably performed the parts assigned to them in the programme, when the dignified president announced that the time had now arrived when they were to elect a new set of officers.

This, indeed, was no trifling matter. The importance of the result necessitated the taking of unusual precautions. Two tellers were appointed to collect and count the eleven ballots. Their every action was scrutinized in order to see that there was no fraudulent voting. When each had voted, and the result for president ascertained, it was duly announced by the secretary, Miss Tillie Gump, as follows: Gottlieb Greenschnable, one vote; Shadrach Doolittle, three votes; Philip Henry Dudelsack, five votes; blank two. Dr. Philip Henry Dudelsack was, therefore, declared elected president of the —— Literary Society for the ensuing term of three months, and a committee of two was appointed to conduct him to the chair—a distance of three and a half feet.

Covered with confusion at this great and unexpected honor, the newly-elected president arose, cleared his throat several times, fixed his eyes first on the table, then on a crack in the ceiling, and finally on a figure on the wall paper directly in front of him, and then launched out into a speech, in which he expressed gratitude for the honor conferred upon him and promised to discharge the duties of the office to the best of his ability, winding up with the remark: "That, whilst I am satisfied that there are others here that are far better qualified than I am, still. I believe that I can do much better than my immediate predecessor has done."

Fatal words! Though spoken in a spirit of levity, they were destined to sow dissension in the ranks of that unfortunate society and destroy the peace of the whole community. For, piercing the little soul of Shadrach Doolittle, they stirred up all the spite and rancor in his narrow nature, and when at the next meeting he delivered his parting address he denounced his conceited successor in the most bitter terms.

To sit there and hear himself stigmatized as conceited, presumptuous, empty headed, etc., and to know that Arabella Stites, Tillie Gump and Fanny Winn were listening to those slanderous words, was almost more than Philip Henry could bear. His feelings were wrought up to such a pitch that, like a slumbering volcano, they threatened to burst forth at any moment and overwhelm his traducer; but, fortunately for Shadrach, the dignity of Philip's position forced him to repress his indignation and bear the insult in silence.

On the adjournment of the society the young ladies went upstairs to don their wraps. There was then a general outburst of feeling.

"It's a downright shame for that gawky old Shad Doolittle to talk like that!" exclaimed Tillie Gump. "I'd a knocked him down, if I'd a been Phil."

"He served Phil just right!" interrupted Fanny Winn. "What business had he to say what he did, anyhow?"

"Well, he was just in fun, and if Shad wasn't such a conceited fool, he'd a taken it that way, and not a made such a holy show of himself as he did to-night. I don't intend to speak to the mean old thing again as long as I live."

"Well, you can do just as you please, Tillie Gump, but I haven't any use for that stuck-up peacock, Phil Dudelsack; have you, Miss Stites?"

"Oh, you needn't ask her; everybody knows she's sweet on Shad."

Stung to the quick by Shadrach's spiteful thrusts, and all the resentment in his fiery nature aroused, Philip spent several days in vainly seeking some vulnerable point where Shadrach might be successfully attacked, and when he had about given up all hope, a fortunate accident revealed a weak place which he believed would enable him to be surely and speedily revenged.

He had been to the blacksmith shop of Mr. Gump and was leisurely returning. His way led past the school which had been dismissed just as he reached it. As he bowed to the teacher, Arabella, something in her pleasant smile prompted him to wait for her till she reached the road. The path leading up to Doolittle's was rough and steep, and now that it was covered with snow and ice was well-nigh impassable; so they went farther up the road and, climbing over a low place in the fence, started up through the long meadow that was commanded by the windows of the Dudelsack homestead. As they trudged along over the slippery ground, his strong arm supporting her whenever they came to a difficult place, and even after all such places had been passed, she incidently remarked

79

that Shadrach was studying for a teacher's certificate, with the intention of applying for the place now occupied by Mr. Johnston, whose term would expire in June.

When he left her at Doolittle's gate, he went straight to the barn, where he pranced back and forth shaking his fist at various objects and muttering to himself: "Nice scheme—very nice, indeed—get the school—court all day—maybe he will—I'll fix him," etc.

In perfecting his plans he lingered about the barn till he was called to supper.

Noticing his preoccupied manner as he sat down to the table, his mother asked: "Why, Philip, what are you studying about?"

"Oh, about Arabella Stites," volunteered Polly Ann in that irritating tone of voice peculiar to her.

"How do you know what I am thinking about?"

"Oh, maybe I didn't see her coming up through Doolittle's meadow this afternoon, and maybe I didn't see some one's arm around her as they poked along; oh no, maybe I didn't."

"Well, what if you did?"

"Oh, nothing, only I wouldn't try to cut Shad out if I were you."

"Who's trying to cut him out?"

"Oh, nobody, of course; it didn't look that way, did it?"

"Well, suppose it did, what then?"

"Oh nothing, only I think you'd better see your way clear to making a living before you think of cutting any-one out"

"Well, you are a nice one to give that kind of advice, when you and your squalling brats have to sponge off of mother half of the time, because old Blodgett can't make a living for you."

"Now, look here, Philip Henry! If mother asks me to come here and help her, what business is it of yours?"

"Help her? Well, that's rich! It looks like helping her, doesn't it, when she has to be up night after night till after midnight, trying to get one or the other of your howling brats to go to sleep. I don't want any of that kind of help in mine, I assure you."

"Mother!" exclaimed Polly Ann, bursting into tears, "I never thought when you asked me to come out here that I was to be insulted by that great big overgrown thing!"

"That'll do, Philip," interposed the mother. "I don't want to hear any more of that kind of talk; not another word."

"Well, then let her keep her oar out of my affairs."

To prevent the recurrence of these little pleasantries and to avoid his mother's displeasure, Philip, from this time on, ate his meals in silence, and spent his leisure moments either in the barn or locked up in his room, where almost every night he could be heard pacing to and fro till quite a late hour.

This condition of affairs had continued for a week or more, when one evening, as the mother and the two daughters were gathered about the stove in the sitting-room, Polly Ann said:

"Ma, I think Phil must be up to something, for he looks awful serious, and you know how little he eats, and how close he keeps to his room. As I passed his door last night I heard him saying over and over to himself, 'common and uncommon, proper and improper.' I haven't the least idea what he meant. And then, this morning as Susan was sitting in the covered carriage in the barn, she saw him shaking his fist at the door and muttering something about getting even with him. I suppose he meant Shad; and I think, ma, you ought to speak to him."

"If you wouldn't aggravate him, Polly, he'd be all right."

"Me aggravate him!" exclaimed Polly, with an injured air; "you wouldn't say that if you only had heard all the tantalizing things he's said to me."

"What did he say?"

"I don't wish to repeat them, ma," replied Polly Ann, with a look that left the impression that though she was a very much abused person, she was altogether too kind hearted to retaliate.

In spite of the frequent importunities of Polly Ann, his mother refused to remonstrate with him, and he continued to keep up those mysterious mutterings in his room and to perform his daily pantomime in the barn to an audience of one in the covered carriage.

On going after the mail one morning, Philip found in his box a letter addressed in a strange hand. After critically examining the envelope for several moments, he opened it and drew forth one of those works of art—a comic valentine.

When he saw the villainous picture and read the vile rhymes attached, his face looked like he was suffering from an acute attack of erysipelas.

Crumpling the missive in his hand and thrusting it into his pocket, he impatiently mounted his horse, which, accustomed to leisurely saunter home whilst his rider perused the daily paper, was considerably surprised at being continually urged into a gallop by repeated cuts of a switch, and even as he was being put into the stall he watched Philip over his shoulder, apparently amazed at his unusual conduct and sulphurous language.

Leaving the barn he entered the house and went to

his room. When he reappeared a few minutes later with a shotgun on his shoulder, his faithful dog bounded for joy, but when he discharged both barrels in the air without any game being in sight, the dog squatted down and looked up into Philip's face with a perplexed air; and, as he saw him reload the gun with a double quantity of the largest-sized shot, his rapidly vibrating tail ceased to wag and lay motionless on the ground.

With the heavily charged piece on his shoulder, Philip stalked moodily out of the yard and down the road, followed by the dog, and from the slinking gait of the latter he was evidently aware that mischief was brewing and was heartily ashamed of the part he was taking.

Abner Doolittle had just come down to his front gate as the pair reached it, and giving them an inquiring look, he said:

" Good morning, Phil. Want to see Shad?"

" Yes."

" Well, he went to town early this morning to get examined, and may not be back till late. Did you want anything particular?"

" No!" abruptly said Philip, as he turned and left.

Followed by Doolittle's inquisitive eyes, they went on down the road till a bend hid them from view, when they took a short cut through a stone quarry and the woods beyond to the meadow in the rear of the barn. Once more at home Philip put away his gun and busied himself in performing several chores, which in his excitement were forgotten.

Nothing further occurred until the next Friday afternoon when, as he was returning from the blacksmith shop, Philip again accidentally reached the school just as it was being dismissed, and, of course, accompanied Arabella home. This time, however, they took the steep and slippery path instead of the meadow, for, while taking them out of the range of Polly Ann's vision, it also enabled him to extend a helping hand rather oftener than the other would have done. As they sauntered slowly along, Philip unconcernedly asked :

" How did Shad get along with his examination ? "

" Oh, all right. He has his certificate and expects to get the school, for his father expects to be re-elected, and as he has the promise of Mr. Van Duzen's vote, he's pretty certain to get it."

" I hope he may," sneered Philip, under his breath, and immediately changed the subject.

When he vented his feelings in the barn that evening one would have thought from his actions that he was in training for a baseball match, a prize fight or some other equally sanguinary contest. Even his pet coon, alarmed at his wild gesticulations and startled at the upsetting of a barrel of grain, scampered down stairs and took refuge under a manger. During this pantomime he was continually muttering : " Confound it—got his certificate, did he—will get the school, will he— dead sure of it, is he— well, may be he will—old Doolittle be re-elected, will he—I'll see about it."

The next afternoon found Philip in the shop of Mr. Gump, who in a small way was the political " boss " of the neighborhood.

With his foot resting on one corner of the forge, he had been watching the hammering of a glowing piece of iron, and now that it had been returned to the fire and Mr. Gump had resumed his place at the bellows handle, Philip asked :

" I wonder where Mr. Johnston will teach next year ?"

" Why, is he going to leave?"

" Why, I thought it was understood that Shad Doolittle was to have the place."

" You did, eh; who told you ? "

" Why, old Doolittle feels sure of being re-elected, and says Van Duzen has promised to vote for Shad, and I suppose you will also."

" Well, maybe he'll be re-elected, and maybe he won't," said Gump, with a peculiar twinkle in his eye.

" Why, who intends to run against him ? "

" Well, it might be Mr. Winn, and then again it mightn't."

" Is he likely to vote for Shad ? "

" Now, see here, Phil, are you very anxious for him to get the school ? "

" Well, no, not very."

" Well, you do all you can for Winn and Shad'll not get it."

From the number of long and confidential conversations held during the next week with several doubtful voters, it was evident that Philip was seeing about it with a vengeance.

Now, Polly Ann, whose bilious disposition had been stirred up by her brother's caustic remarks, had resolved to oppose him in any and all schemes, and it is, therefore, not at all strange that these mysterious visits did not escape her watchful eyes, and that her surmises as to their probable cause were tolerably correct; nor is it surprising that ·in her desire to circumvent him she should go to these same voters and endeavor to counteract what he had said, and that on the Sunday before the election she should have her submissive husband running his rheumatic legs off on the same errand.

At the appointed hour on the next Monday an earnest little group of citizens assembled at the district school house. and at the exact moment prescribed by law proceeded to discharge the solemn duty of electing a school director. by first selecting a judge and clerk of election. The choice. by no means unanimous. fell on Philip Henry Dudelsack and Dominicus Goodfellow respectively.

When the election officers had taken their places and the ballot box. an empty cigar box. had been opened and held up to view to prove that it was empty, the voting commenced. As each of the assembled citizens — conscious of his own honesty and integrity. yet doubtful of that of his neighbor — felt it incumbent upon himself to see that the purity of the ballot was maintained. the course of each ballot as it traveled from the voter's hand to the slit in the box was followed by the eyes of all.

When they gathered around the election officers at the close of the polls to witness the counting of the ballots. each was satisfied that. no matter what the result of the election might be. the election had been fair and honest. Yet few. however. were prepared for the actual result: for when the last vote had been counted, it was found that Abner Doolittle had received nineteen and Theophilus Winn thirty-four votes. This, when a majority of five was considered large. was looked upon as an overwhelming defeat for Abner Doolittle.

When the news of the result spread through the neighborhood. it stirred up a tremendous commotion. The community was rent into two factions that. from denouncing the principals in the affair. soon fell to vilifying each other. The defeated candidate. who said he had not wanted the office and had only consented to run at the earnest solicitation of some of his neighbors. was loud in his denunciation of Philip as the cause of his downfall.

The literary society. as may be expected. did not

escape the general infection. The next meeting was held on the night of the election, and was stormy indeed. Each of the members taking sides on the question, the feeling ran so high that the exercises set down in the programme were postponed, and the society went into the election of officers, the result for president being as follows: Philip Henry Dudelsack, one; Gottlieb Greenschnable, three; Shadrach Doolittle, one; Ballot-box Stuffer, one; Wire Puller, one; Fraud, one; Boodle Gang, one; and scattering, one.

II.

From the clouds that lowered upon the brows of the Doolittle household as they took their accustomed places at the breakfast table on the morning after the election for school director, it was very evident that stormy weather would soon prevail. As Abner asked a stereotyped blessing over a plate of fried bacon, his face was particularly gloomy; that of his wife was no brighter, and the malicious gleam that occasionally lit up the anything but handsome face of Shadrach, like the lightning playing about the approaching storm, was ominous indeed.

The calm following the conclusion of Abner's devotions was of short duration, for Deborah had barely ceased pouring out the coffee when she turned to Shadrach and said:

"Son, I don't want you to have anything more to do with that sneaking Phil Dudelsack, as there is no telling what he might take a notion to do."

"Pooh! Do you think I'm afraid of that coward?"

"You can't be too careful, son, for 'Mandy Dingfelter says he always carries a knife and two pistols with him."

"Well, he can't scare me with his knife and pistols, and I intend to get even with him; you see if I don't."

"Son!" interrupted the father, "I don't want you to get mixed up in any dispute with him, for he'll get his just deserts soon enough. If he keeps on acting as he did at the election, it won't be long till he'll land in the penitentiary."

"Why, what did he do at the election?" innocently asked Arabella.

"Why, enough to land him in jail, if I were a mind to prosecute him."

"In jail! Why, did you see him do anything?" queried Arabella, who did not now hesitate to take sides, believing as she did that she had nothing further to fear from Abner Doolittle's political influence.

"He didn't have to see it," interrupted Shadrach. "Who ever heard of such a one-sided election in this precinct? Why, twenty-six different persons told me that they had voted for pap, but when the votes were counted he only had nineteen! Why, a blind man could see that dirty work had been done: and who else could have done it but that miserable, low-lived sneak across the way? You mark my word, I'll make him pay dearly for it before a year rolls around."

"You must surely be mistaken, for though he is a little hotheaded, I hardly believe he would be guilty of what you accuse him."

"You impudent hussy!" exclaimed Deborah, with flashing eyes. "How dare you sit there and take the part of that sneak, who does everything he can to humiliate my son?"

"If your son could have perceived that what Dr. Dudelsack said was only intended to be taken in fun, he need not have been humiliated," replied Arabella, undis mayed by Deborah's belligerent attitude.

"Well, I don't propose to let anybody insult me and then say it was only in fun," said Shadrach, bringing his fist down on the table with a bang that made the dishes dance.

"That's right, my son!" exclaimed the father, forgetting in his excitement the cautious advice he had given but a moment before. "I glory in your spunk!"

"Now, pap, you hadn't ought to egg him on that way. You know you don't want to have him dirty his hands with that lying, sneaking, thieving—"

"Your remarks," interrupted Arabella, "are entirely—"

"What! You little hussy!" shrieked Deborah, turning on the school teacher. "You must be setting your cap for that sneak the way you stand up for him, and I want you to understand, right now, that the sooner you pack up your traps and get out of here the better."

"I'm not at all anxious to remain, I assure—"

"Will you defy me, you—"

"There now, ma, don't allow yourself to get excited," interposed Shad. "You know you are apt to have another spell"

"Spell! I don't care if I have forty spells. I don't propose to have a sassy school teacher talk that way to me!"

"Now, ma," repeated Shad.

"Don't talk to me. You don't care anything for me, or you wouldn't sit there and hear me insulted by that impudent little—little—little spitfire!"

There is no knowing what might have been the result of Deborah's frenzy, had not Arabella at this juncture quietly left the room. As it was, however, she did not escape a spell, and there was soon great hurrying and scurrying on the part of Abner and his two sons to get the camphor bottle and the valerian mixture.

When Arabella left the table she repaired to her room, where she immediately began to pack all of her belongings in her trunk. This done she donned her wraps and, leaving the house by the front door, started on her way to school.

She had gone but a short distance and was picking her way carefully along the slippery path when, as she passed a hay stack, she was confronted by the angular Shadrach.

Without appearing to notice him, she was about to proceed on her way when he blurted out:

" I say, Miss Stites, you mustn't mind what ma says."

" Why ? "

" Why, 'cause I want you and she to be good friends."

" It is a matter of indifference to me what your mother's feelings are."

" But it isn't to me."

" Why ? "

" Well, just this. I've been waiting till I got a school before I said anything. I expect to get a school soon, and then I—then I—expect to get married," said Shadrach, as he moved about uneasily.

" Well, what has that to do with your mother and me ? "

" Well, you see, it would be kind of unpleasant to marry a girl that ma didn't like."

" Yes, I suppose it would."

" Well, then, I want you and ma to make up, for we will want to live at home for a while."

"I don't see what your mother's feelings toward me have to do with you and your wife living at home."

"You don't?" said Shadrach, with some surprise. "Why, it's you I want to marry."

"Oh, indeed! You are getting very humorous all of a sudden."

"No, I am in dead earnest."

"Oh, but you are. I never suspected that you could be so humorous. Instead of trying to get a school, you ought to write for the comic papers."

"Are you making fun of me?"

"Why, by no means!"

"Well, why don't you give me an answer?" impatiently asked Shadrach, growing red in the face.

"You really do not know how funny you are. If you would only write for the comic papers, you would at once become famous. There are so few real humorists that there is a large field open. The majority of readers, you know, prefer the humorous and comic to the serious and tragic."

"Well, you know I—"

"Of course, I know that you are modest, like all great men, but then if you will only make the attempt success will be assured."

"But that isn't what I—"

"Of course, I know that geniuses do not always appreciate their talents, and that they aspire to something for which they have no particular bent," said Arabella, talking so rapidly that Shadrach could hardly get a word in edgeways. "There is Dore, for instance, who had no peer as an illustrator of books, and yet who was exceedingly anxious to become a great landscape painter."

"Now, look here! I'm not trifling," exclaimed

Shadrach, whose temperature was rapidly approaching the boiling point.

"No, no; certainly not. But you really do not appreciate your talent for rich and irresistible humor. You ought to lose no time in getting started. But I must hurry on to school, as it is getting late. Tell your ma that I will send for my trunk and will not again annoy her with my presence."

With that she sprang past him and hurried on her way, leaving him to mutter and grind his teeth in impotent rage.

She did not slacken her pace till she reached the low place in the fence separating the field from the road, and did not stop to catch her breath till she was safe in the road.

She had hardly begun to breathe naturally when she heard some one approaching, and as she apprehensively turned to see who it was, she saw Philip coming down the road, with a valise in one hand and an umbrella in the other.

As he came to where she stood and saw her flushed face, he said something about her being in an unusual hurry to get to school, especially as there was plenty of time to spare.

"Oh," said she, "I thought it was late." And then, as she noticed the valise, she paled somewhat as she asked: "Are you going to leave us?"

"Yes; I am now on my way to the city, and I will leave for Chicago this evening."

"To Chicago?" said Arabella, growing still paler.

"Yes. An old schoolmate of mine has been practicing there for several years, but his health has failed and he has asked me to take charge of his practice while he goes to California to recuperate."

" Does he expect to be gone long ? "

" Probably a year."

" Then you have given up the idea of resuming practice in the city ? "

" Yes; I want to get away from here. I begin to see that in the part I have taken in the events of the past few months, that I have made an ass and a laughing-stock of myself, and I want to go some place where I will not be subjected to the ridicule of certain people."

" You put entirely too much stress on what has recently happened. You are too easily discouraged.. You have friends here, and warm ones at that."

" Where are they ? I don't believe there is any one here who cares whether I stay or go."

" Oh, you are certainly mistaken. You take an altogether too gloomy a view of the situation."

" No, I think not. I must be going, as I have several matters to arrange which will keep me busy all day. I hope, however, that as I am probably leaving this locality for good, that I do not carry your ill will with me."

" My ill will ? Why should I cherish any ill will toward you ? " said Arabella, with illy-disguised surprise.

" Why, you know, it is said that I was instrumental in securing Abner Doolittle's defeat."

" Yes."

" And thereby destroyed Shadrach's prospects of getting the school."

" Yes."

" Well, I thought that you might cherish some resentment at my—"

" On the contrary, I am very thankful indeed that he did not get it ! "

" Why, I thought—"

" What ? "

" That you were very much interested in—in—"

" Shadrach Doolittle ? "

" Yes."

" What made you think so ? "

" Why, that's what I've heard reported."

" The reports were without any foundation whatever. I have not the slightest interest in the Doolittle family; in fact, I have left their house for good."

"Indeed !" said Philip, surprised in turn. " Why, how was that ? "

" His mother called me some very hard names when I took your part at the breakfast table this morning."

" Then I have at least one friend," said Philip, as he eyed her intently.

"Oh," said Arabella, as she colored slightly and bent her eyes to the ground, " I don't believe in keeping my mouth shut when any one is being misrepresented."

" Then it was only your sense of justice, and not any feeling for me, that prompted your defense ? "

Arabella grew redder and said nothing, and Philip stood there a few moments mutely looking at her. Suddenly he dropped his valise to the ground, caught her in his arms and pressed a kiss on her lips.

As he did so she looked up in his face and simply said : " Oh, doctor."

When they parted a few minutes later, she to hurry to school and he to the city, they each carried happy hearts and smiling faces.

The rest of our story is soon told. Philip was soon installed in the office of his old schoolmate, who then took his departure for California in search of health, only to find a resting place in that narrow house built by the sexton.

The practice in Philip's hands grew and increased so

rapidly that ere the end of a year he felt justified in making a flying trip to Cincinnati and claiming the hand of Arabella in marriage.

Shadrach, on the other hand, is still a bachelor, partly because he has never been able to get a school and earn enough to support a wife, and partly because he has not been able to find any young woman who has the courage to attempt to live with his " ma."

—————

DOCTOR POTTS' THEORY.

To Doctor Potts, through long research,
　　There came a brilliant thought
Which seem'd, for poor untutored man,
　　With much importance fraught.

" Why study years and years," said he,
　　" Till brain and body tir'd.
When all the knowledge in the world
　　Could be at once acquir'd?"

He then began to seek a case
　　His theory to prove,
And every quibble, fear or doubt,
　　From skeptic minds remove.

Dame Fortune soon a subject brought ;
　　A man with broken head
Was found upon the street one night
　　And given up for dead.

95

The doctor drew the broken bones
    From out the ghastly rent,
Then deep into the cerebrum
    A hypodermic sent.

The patient then was put to bed,
    But when the morning broke
Uneasily he turned his head
    And from his stupor woke.

The doctor said he must not read
    Until the wound had heal'd,
But when it did, oh then there was
    A wondrous change reveal'd.

Long since he had read each book they brought;
    The paper, too, was stale,
And though they pointed to the date,
    It was of no avail.

They brought him books fresh from the press,
    But still his anger grew;
He thought they were but joking him
    And called for something new.

They told him stories long and short,
    And cracked the newest jokes;
But to him they were old, so he drove them out
    With fierce and heavy strokes.

He left the house and straightway went
    To see the latest play,
But soon he found it was not new
    And quickly went his way.

He then tried books, both large and small,
    In Greek and French and Dutch,
On philosophy, microscopy,
    Theosophy and such.

Anatomy and botany,
    And anthropology,
Astronomy, phlebotomy
    And every 'ology;

Yet found he could not gratify
    His wish for something new,
As everything that could be learned
    He now already knew.

So growing tired of such a life,
    He then in sheer despair
Just took sufficient arsenic
    To end his sad career.

POSTSCRIPT.

When Doctor Potts the sequel heard,
    And view'd the clammy corse,
He did not long survive the shock,
    So keen was his remorse.

THE STORY OF A POEM.

John Regenschirm was a self-made man, who was particularly proud of his own handiwork.

He had cultivated the faculty of gaining wealth to the exclusion of all others. Music had no charms for him, and as for literature, it was his proud boast that he didn't "read no poetry nor no novels." He considered all such literature frivolous, foolish and effeminate in the extreme. His reading was confined to the pages of the daily newspaper. The markets, weather, and occasionally politics, were the only features possessing any attraction for him. He had no time for the balance, even if he had been inclined to read them.

He had retired from business with the intention of spending the remainder of his days in ease, which, however, was not such an easy matter as he had anticipated. For a time he went down town every day to mingle with his former business associates, but they were as eager in the pursuit of wealth as he had been and had no time to devote to him. He realized that he was now no longer as prominent a figure as he had been, but was like a useless piece of driftwood, buffeted about in the busy stream. These reflections were not very consoling, and consequently his visits to the city gradually grew less and less frequent.

He remained at home more and read the paper more thoroughly. He read every scrap of political news. He even read the horrible details of several murders and railroad accidents. One day he became deeply interested in a circumstantial account of the hairbreadth escapes of a noted detective. Now it so happened that just below this narrative was a short poem. The poem had no connection or relation whatever to the preceding tale, yet he unconsciously read the first verse of it before he realized what he was doing. When it dawned on him that he had actually been reading poetry he indignantly cast the paper aside. His curiosity, however, had been excited, and he soon picked it up again. He did not want to give in all at once, so he tried very hard to read an article on the "Tariff on Wool," but it was no use, so he capitulated and read the poem. He read it not only once, but several times, and also noted the name and address of the author. It even made such an impression on him that he was tempted to cut it out and preserve it, but he feared that the mutilated paper might betray his actions and give others an excuse to twit him. He read and reread it, however, till he had committed it to memory, and when he went down town the next day he bought another copy of the paper, cut out the poem and placed it in his pocket-book.

The tone of the poem seemed to indicate a feeling of despondency on the part of the writer, and from reading it so often he began to be curious as to the author and to wonder just what kind of an individual he might be, and whether or not he felt as much dissatisfied with his condition as he did.

He had been turning the matter over in his mind for a couple of weeks, when it occurred to him that as the poet's home was less than three hours' ride by rail distant, he might take the morning train, make a flying trip, satisfy his curiosity and get back the same day, without his absence exciting suspicion.

The next day but one he put his plan into execution.

On arriving at his destination he was somewhat uncertain as to the best plan of pursuing his inquiries, as he was averse to attracting too much attention, so he stepped into the waiting-room of the station and sat down to deliberate on the matter.

While sitting there several citizens, who had come to the station to see the train pass by, also came in and sat down to rest and recover from their excitement. As luck would have it, their conversation turned on the very subject of most interest to Regenschirm. One of the villagers made a disparaging remark concerning the poet and another replied in defense, saying that even if he did nothing but write poetry and invent useless machines, while his mother was obliged to take in sewing in order to make a living, that he had a good heart, and then reminded the first speaker how he had helped to nurse the Peterson children when they had the diptheria and none of the neighbors would go near them, although the father and mother had been sitting up night after night and were completely tired out.

This was a hint for Regenschirm, and without waiting for a second one he left the station and made his way into the village. He had no difficulty in finding the house he was looking for, as it was pointed out to him by the first person he asked.

On reaching the front gate and seeing a shock-headed, dreamy-looking individual sitting on the porch, he was for a moment somewhat disconcerted, and not being certain whether that was the person he was after or not, he inquired:

" Does Mr. Aufschneider live here ? "

" No, sir; there is no one of that name living in the village."

" There must be some mistake then, for I wanted to see him in regard to an invention and was directed to this house."

"Perhaps I am the person you are seeking. Wil you come in?"

Taking a vacant seat on the porch, Regenschirm declared his mission by explaining that he was nearly seventy years old, that he had earned his own living ever since he was ten years old, that he had attended strictly to business and had "never read no poetry or no novels."

"What objection have you to poetry?"

"Why, it's all tomfoolery and poppycock. I've heard people reading it and for the life of me I couldn't see any sense in it. The idea of saying a little child's smile could melt an icy heart."

"Why, what is wrong with that?"

"What is wrong? Why, who ever heard of a live man with a frozen heart? Why, it's all nonsense. It's all bosh! It isn't possible! If a man has anything to say, let him say it in plain English, so everybody can understand it."

"Then you would have everything plain and without ornament?"

"Yes, that's just it. That's my style exactly."

"You would raise hay in your front yard, instead of grass and flowers?"

"No, I don't mean that, but—"

"You would have no pictures on your walls, no curtains at your windows, no figures in your carpets?"

"That isn't what I—"

"You'd dress your wife and children like Quakers?"

"No, you don't understand. Flowers and pictures and nice clothes are all right, but—"

"If they are all right, then why is it wrong for us to ornament our language in the same manner? Why is it wrong for us to cultivate the imagination, so that the poorest and meanest may see beauties in the life about them that will give them nobler ideas and make them purer and better?"

"Imagination doesn't buy bread and butter."

"Perhaps not, but it enables its possessor to derive pleasures from his humble surroundings which were never dreamed of by those without imagination, and which can not help being elevating and refining in their tendency."

Seeing that he was not making any headway in proving the absurdity of poetry, Regenschirm reverted to the subject of invention, in which he pretended to be considerably interested.

Enthusiastic on this, as he was on the previous subject, the poet and inventor invited his guest to visit his workshop. The room, not very large, was filled with models of all sorts, from a miniature flying machine to a mouse trap.

In one corner was a rude model of a machine which had just been completed and in which Regenschirm at once became interested. The more he examined it the more he became satisfied that it embodied valuable features, and when he was obliged to take his departure it was with the promise of returning in a few days

He had become as much interested in the machine as he had in the poem, and in a short time succeeded in getting others interested in it to such an extent that a stock company was organized, which bought the patent and paid the inventor a sum far in excess of his most sanguine expectations.

The poet's mother now no longer takes in sewing, but lives comfortably with her gifted son in their neat little home. All of which goes to show that a man may be of some use in this world even if he does occasionally write poetry and have it published in the daily papers.

THE AMENITIES OF THE SICKROOM.

When burning with fever and racked with pain,
   'Tis then so very nice
To have a dozen aged dames
   To give me good advice.

To have one say how badly I look,
   And gloomily shake her head,
As she tells of a friend with the same disease
   Who now, alas, is dead.

And how it soothes my shattered nerves,
   And drives my pain away,
To tell each one just how I feel
   Five hundred times a day.

And then the mixtures I must take,
   The plasters I endure,
The lotions, pills and powders, too,
   And each a sovereign cure.

Ah, yes, these dear, benevolent dames,
   I love each one so well
That I'd like to explode a dynamite bomb
   And land them all in—heaven.

AN ALLEGORICAL DREAM.

I seemed to be walking in the middle of a street, lined on either side by tall buildings.

About two hundred yards in advance, and going in the same direction, was another man.

Still farther beyond was a small, black object, which I took to be a kitten, and which, when the pedestrian had come within ten yards of it, sprang toward him.

Frightened at its aggressive conduct, the man turned and fled, pursued by the animal, which increased in size at each bound till it towered above its victim, and fell upon him, when within a few yards of where I stood, and tore him to pieces.

Transfixed with horror and amazement, I stood like a statue, eyeing the fierce monster, which, satisfied that its victim was dead, was now approaching me.

To flee was certain death, so, firmly grasping my heavy cane and flourishing it before me, I made a step forward, when lo! the beast paused, and, as I advanced, began to retreat, though still facing me. Continuing to advance, it continued to retreat, and grew smaller and smaller. Pressing on past the bleeding corpse, the beast steadily diminished in size, till, on reaching its starting place, it suddenly disappeared.

In surprise, I looked in every direction to discover whence it had flown, but could see no trace of it.

In looking around, I saw an old man leaning out of an upper window in one of the buildings, and, thinking he might explain the mystery, I asked him what this strange beast might be called.

After contemplating me for a few moments, he said it was called CALUMNY.

IN DEFENSE OF MANKIND.

When I hear of those who are all too prone
  Their fellow-men to asperse ;
Who loudly declare, when they read of a crime :
  " We are going from bad to worse ;"

Who boldly assert, with an air which says,
  " Dispute it, if you can,"
That every one knows the dog and the horse
  Are better, far, than man ;

It is then that I think these pessimists
  Have never received a hint
Of the thousands of kind and praiseworthy deeds
  Which do not appear in print.

And when they point to noble acts
  Performed by a wretched cur,
I doubt if they know they're published, because
  It's so seldom they occur.

With eyes for naught but the sins of men,
  They are like unto carrion crows
That pass over what is pure and sweet
  For that which offends the nose.

CHILDHOOD DAYS.

Oh give me back my childhood days,
　With their fictions believ'd to be true,
When the ragman carried off all bad boys,
　And Santa Claus came down the flue;

When mother would cry whene'er I was hurt,
　And cure me at once with a kiss:
When abundance of jam and ginger-cake
　Was the acme of earthly bliss;

When I rode about on my father's back,
　Who pranced quite vigorously,
And I felt that none in all the earth
　Were as wise or as good as he;

When I thought it wicked to tell a lie,
　And worse to steal a pin,
And had never a hint that this beautiful world
　Could be so full of sin.

Yes, give me back my childhood days,
　From guile and hypocrisy free,
When I rode about on my father's back,
　And shouted in childish glee.

ALONE.

I'm jostl'd about by the hurrying throng
  That ebbs and flows through the busy streets;
And everywhere I cast my eyes
  My glance but cold indifference meets.

All are absorbed in their own affairs,
  And none from the beaten path depart
To soothe my sorrow, ease my pain,
  Or help me bear my heavy heart.

Not he who is cast on the desert isle,
  Or doomed to lie in the dungeon cell,
Can feel as lonely as I have felt,
  Or half as sad a tale can tell.

LIFE'S BATTLEFIELD.

Oh, painter, when in thy happiest mood,
  Depict for me life's battlefield;
Yet not the corse, or the bleaching skull,
  But, rather, the flowers 'neath which they're conceal'd.

AUTOGRAPHS.

Ha, ha! Ho, ho! It makes me laugh
To think you'd want my autograph.

———

As fickle as a weather-vane,
    As restless as a thistledown,
As full of moods as an April day,
———   And always looks out for number *One.
*A coquette, aged sixteen.

——— —

An autograph? That's all you want?
    Why, bless your little heart,
To think to write a verse or two,
    Requires so little art.
You'll have to come another day,
    I'm very much afraid;
My book of poems I can not find,
    My "specs" have been mislaid.

———

Go seek through all the world;
    Through palace and through hovel,
And you'll scarce find so young a *girl
———   To write so big a novel.
*An aspiring miss, aged thirteen years, who began writing a
novel, but never finished the first chapter.

——— —

FAME.

'Tis by degrees of light and shade
That lives of mortals are portrayed;
Yet only when extremes contrast,
Do they the public gaze arrest.

THE LONG-TAILED RAT AND THE DAPPER MOUSE.

Come, children, and gather around my knee,
And listen to what I shall tell to thee.
'Tis a tale of woe and fortune's whim
That's quite as true as those of Grimm.

Long, long ago, when fairies were seen
To dance upon the village green,
'Tis said there lived in a tiny house
A handsome, charming lady mouse.

Her fame, which spread both far and wide,
Brought scores of suitors to her side.
From every clime and every land
They came to claim her dainty hand.

Among the throng was a dapper mouse
Who hoped that she might be his spouse,
And brought to his aid, in his efforts to win,
The tones evoked from a violin.

The charming lady, to tell the truth,
Seemed well disposed toward the youth:
But into the fire went all of his fat,
When on to the scene came a long-tailed rat.

The rat was accomplished and handsome they say;
There wasn't an instrument he couldn't play;
Then the verses he wrote, and his deep bass voice,
Decided at once the fair lady's choice.

Alas! for the mouse so dapper and sleek,
He grew morose inside of a week,
And said what dreadful things he would do,
And raised an awful hullabaloo.

The long-tailed rat settled down with his wife
To enjoy the rest of his natural life;
And in spite of the mouse's furious rage
They lived in peace to a ripe old age.

THE DESERTED MILL.

Thy crumbling stack and moldering walls
A scene of long ago recalls,
When people came from far and near
The music of thy voice to hear,
And brought the grain of golden hue
Which in this fertile region grew;
But now, alas! that voice is hush'd,
Thy pride has been completely crush'd,
For he whom thou hast wealthy made
To other scenes long since has stray'd.
Thy services were soon forgot,
And thou wert left to die and rot.

SHADOWS.

The shadows we see on a summer day
So swiftly over the meadow play,
Are like the grief which wrings our hearts,
Yet makes us glad when it departs.

THE COMBINATION.

There was a young woman in our town
   Who aspired to be a poet,
As her mind was a garden of beautiful thoughts,
   And she wanted the world to know it.

She read every poem that she could find,
   Its style and figures dissected;
She studied its rhythm, its meter and feet,
   To learn how they were constructed.

But all she saw was letters and points—
   So few, indeed, 'twas surprising—
That she thought in them she had found at last
   The secret of improvising.

She began at once to try her hand,
   But found, to her aggravation,
She never, no matter how much she tried,
   Could hit the combination.

THE VIOLET'S PLAINT.

The poet was wont, in times gone by,
To praise my shrinking modesty;
But now, a slave to fashion's whim,
'Tis bold effrontery pleases him.

————

A RARE GIFT.

As each succeeding year grows old,
    And Christmas closer draws,
My vagrant thoughts unbidden turn
    To dear old Santa Claus.

My stocking by the fireside hung
    I hope that he will find,
And in its very bottom place
    A gift of rarest kind.

'Tis not to gold or precious stones
    To which I now refer;
'Tis neither glory, honor, fame,
    But something better far.

A pair of magic spectacles
    To wear upon my nose,
That I may see the joys of life,
    And not its many woes.

That I may pass my days in peace,
    And envy be forgot;
To live unto the very end
    Contented with my lot.

A SYNONYM.

With spiderlike patience I've carefully search'd
My copy of "Crabb" from cover to cover;
Alas! 'twas in vain that I tried to find
An apt synonym that for X—— might answer.

Affectionate, generous, kind and good,
Sprightly, obliging, sensible, cheerful,
Compassionate, worthy, prudent, sincere,
Amiable, candid, comforting, gentle—
Are some of the words that rewarded my search:
But not one of these will fully describe her,
And so then in order to be understood
I'm obliged to use the sixteen together.

———

A VALENTINE.

A line or two, and nothing more,
  Yet still it serves an end.
If our good wishes it convey
  To some beloved friend.

If some, through envy, malice, hate.
  This day have utilized
To vent their spite on every one
  By whom they've been despis'd,

To no such mean, contemptible
  Intention I incline;
For kindest greetings I would send
  In this, a valentine.

IMAGINATION.

There is a potent talisman
  To human eye unseen,
Yet when I feel its influence
  A change comes o'er the scene.

A fire leaps from my cheerless grate,
  Rich carpets hide the floor,
Whilst on the walls once crack'd and stain'd
  Are paintings by the score.

The light of day through pictured glass
  Sheds many a tinted ray
Upon a nook where rarest books
  In wild profusion lay.

Luxurious ease pervades the scene,
  The lounge invites repose,
And sinking back in sweet content
  I soon begin to doze.

Yet still it falls by far too short;
  Its power though fully spent
Will neither pay my grocer's bills,
  Nor liquidate the rent.

THE FIRST OF APRIL.

How well do I remember
   When I stood at my mother's knee,
And listened in childish wonder
   To this tale of antiquity:
How the fools of every nation,
   Lamenting their many woes,
Were gathered in a queer convention,
   Like a flock of noisy crows;
How impending extermination
   Had so wrought upon their fears
That with many a protestation,
   And an ocean or two of tears,
They sent up a long petition,
   In which they Jove besought
That the Killer's devastation
   Be suddenly brought to naught.
How Jove to their pray'r attended,
   And decreed the Killer should die;
So, as long as time extended,
   They'd increase and multiply;
How they this message hearing,
   Nor paused to offer thanks,
Began, no danger fearing,
   To play their foolish pranks.
And how this day eventful,
   My mother did relate,
Was on the first of April,
   Which they still commemorate.

INDIGENOUS.

A little seed, by the breezes borne,
  A lodging place in my bosom found,
Where glances shot from two bright eyes
  Had made a deep and piercing wound.

Water'd by tears it began to grow,
  And into my heart its rootlets dipp'd;
Its tender branches quickly spread,
  Each with a fragrant blossom tipp'd.

Deeply I breathed their perfume rare,
  And felt it tingle through every vein;
Boundless joy and bliss were mine,
  And gone were every care and pain.

This little plant which has the power
  To change a falcon to a dove,
Or spur us on to noble deeds—
  You ask its name? They call it Love.

————

A SPUNKY MAIDEN.

There was a young man named Fred,
Who a certain young maiden would wed,
  But got full as a goose,
  On some very strong juice,
And had to be put into bed.

This stirr'd up the maiden's spunk;
Of her mind she gave him a chunk,
  And quite forcibly said
  She never would wed
A man who'd go and get—delirious.

WINTER.

When winter swoops down from his home in the North,
　To bluster about like a fierce old brigand,
To kill all the flowers, to drive off the birds,
　And to lock up the streams with his cold, icy hand ;

'Tis then that I sigh for the fragrance of spring,
　For a sight of the cows 'neath the wide spreading tree,
For the musical song of the babbling brook,
　As it hastes on its way to the far distant sea ;

For the hum of the bees, for the bleat of the sheep,
　And the fancies that come on a still summer night ;
And I shudder to think how bleak and how drear
　Are the hills and the valleys in their mantle of white.

Oh, the winter 's for those in the vigor of youth,
　With never a fear of its withering breath ;
But the feeble and old view its coming with dread,
　For to them it is naught but an emblem of death.

THE SCHOOLMA'AM.

Like the genial warmth of spring
  And the cheerful notes of the birds,
Are her bright and pleasant smile
  And her kind and gentle words.

The frail and the tender chords
  In the hearts of those future men
Respond to her delicate touch,
  To vibrate again and again.

Inspired with kindness and love,
  She labors from year to year,
And is doing the noblest work
  Vouchsafed to woman's sphere.

Could we but sit in that school,
  Who've been worn by care and strife,
That our sear'd and wither'd hearts
  Might be quickened anew with life.

NIPPED.

With lofty impulse seiz'd,
  Like Cervantes' errant knight,
I boldly sallied forth
  To set the world aright.

My lance, a caustic pen;
  A trenchant style, my steed;
My armor—thick and strong—
  Unlimited conceit.

*   *   *   *   *   *   *   *

Disheartened, weary, sore,
  At last I've changed my mind.
The cause? Some printed slips:
" Respectfully declined."

BUT WHAT DOES IT ALL AMOUNT TO?

As children, we whine and fret and fuss
If others get more than is given to us;
    But what does it all amount to ?

As scholars, we strive each other to pass
In our eager desire to be first in our class;
    But what does it all amount to ?

As lovers, we rave o'er a pair of bright eyes,
Which we swear have stolen their tints from the skies;
    But what does it all amount to ?

As merchants, we try our pow'r to extend,
And to lay up wealth for others to spend;
    But what does it all amount to ?

As poets, we strike the resounding lyre,
And hope that its echoes may never expire ;
    But what does it all amount to ?

As soldiers, on fame and glory intent,
The blood of mankind in torrents is spent;
    But what does it all amount to ?

As statesmen, we soon into parties divide,
And fiercely berate the opposite side;
    But what does it all amount to ?

Like the snow that melts and passes away,
We live and we die, are forgotten next day,
    And that's about all it amounts to.

www.ingramcontent.com/pod-product-compliance
Lightning Source LLC
Chambersburg PA
CBHW022339020726
47500CB00004B/1187